Tides of Magic

Andi R. Christopher

Sleepy Squid Press

ISBNs:
Paperback: 978-0-473-65762-8
Epub: 978-0-473-65763-5
Mobi: 978-0-473-65764-2

Contents

Chapter One

Charley pulled her car over as far left as she could manage, far enough that she was in the shadow of the pine trees that lined her route, and jabbed her GPS. She'd planned the journey beforehand, and it had seemed something even she could handle; follow the state highway south, turn off towards the sea, and then take the winding coast road north to her destination. She pulled out her phone, which very generously allowed two bars of reception – though still 3G reception – and worked out where she'd gone wrong. She was just at the edge of a headache, her mouth felt dry, and even though she'd showered just hours ago it felt like her skin was crawling with weeks of grime.

She'd meant to set off early, but of course it didn't happen, between a missing shoe and everything else taking inexplicably twice as long as she'd meant it to. She'd always assumed that in an actual emergency she'd miraculously get her shit together, but she'd never really expected to have that put to the test. Now her sister, her sister who had always looked out for her, was missing and somehow Charley still couldn't manage to leave the house before ten, even though Melissa's safety may well depend on it. *What a selfish little girl.*

"Stop it," Charley said aloud to her own self-talk, swinging the car round in the empty road to retrace her journey to the site of her last mistake. These mishaps were always shameful even when she was the only one to witness them. To snap herself out of the put-downs she found a playlist she and Melissa had created together in her sister's last year at home – it was poppy and upbeat, the sort they could dance around Melissa's bedroom singing to, the sort that forced a smile even in the worst times.

Half an hour lost, and Charley was finally heading towards the sea, a river on her right. This was forest and floodplain country, sandwiched between the university city and the rugged lands of the far south. One side of the road was lined with pine trees, while on the other the river caught the glint of the late morning sun. This far south, the air had a cold bite even in the late spring days of early November, but the skies were blue and Charley felt like there was hope.

If she made it to the tiny settlement of Inver Aora, there was some-one there who could help her. According to the on-again-off-again girlfriend of one of her workmate Liam's cousins, anyway. She was more than a little sceptical, but what else could she do? The police were dismissive and her parents more so. And the way her sister had disappeared was weird, verging on impossible, so maybe a weird so-lution from out here in the middle of nowhere would be the one that would actually work.

Charley could only hope so. It didn't feel like she had anyone else on her side.

Their mother's comment that "if one of our children was going to go missing, I'd have thought it would be Charlotte" was a low, spiteful blow, but she couldn't deny there was truth in it. Melissa had her life together – and always had. Melissa was a fifth-year medical student and a *pleasure to be around*. Probably the oddest thing about Melissa was that she loved Charley as much as Charley loved her, had snuck into her room late at night to console her, had sent her goofy texts when she was at uni and Charley was in full-on war with their parents, had helped Charley move to Dunedin, move into her flat when a spare room came up, enrol in uni, enrol in uni again after she dropped out, find a polytech course that might be better suited to her. Melissa had faith in her – she always said things like *less well suited* rather than failure. Well, Charley had let her down once again. She was pretty sure she'd failed again this semester, and she doubted anywhere else would take her.

Truthfully, she wouldn't have minded working late-night shifts in the convenience store for the rest of her life. She didn't care about her parents' expectations; she was an adult now, barely spoke to them, even if it sometimes felt like their voices were echoing through her skull. But she would have liked to make Melissa proud.

And now Melissa was gone. Vanished from her flat just before her fifth-year exams. The door to her bedroom led into the living room where Charley had been gaming into the early hours of the morning, and yet she hadn't heard or seen her leave. Her passport and bank account untouched. Her car, tank half-full, still parked on the street outside. Her phone was by her bed and, unusually, completely out of battery. Charley had recharged it and tried every possible PIN she could think of with no success.

Stress the police had suggested, citing the case of a doctor who vanished from a specialised course decades ago and was never seen again. Rumour had it he'd become an artist in Australia. Art was one of the few things Melissa wasn't good at. *Maybe she needs a break and will be home soon.* But neither the police nor anyone else could explain why there was sea water soaking her desk chair, dripping onto the carpet below.

Charley tensed up at the thought and kept her eyes on the road ahead. There wasn't much traffic now she'd left the state highway, just occasional cars and utes headed west. The road curved and dipped with the shape of the land, the pine forests thinning out, and she caught her first glimpse of the sea. If she'd had her way, she'd have never gone to the coast in her life again. Charley had hated the sea from when she was small – just another way she was *weird* and *difficult* – and could never explain why, only that it made her nauseous, her head heavy, and her whole body ache. She didn't have a choice now, though, and she tried to focus on other things, as the looming deep came ever closer.

Where the road reached the coast was beautiful, even for someone who hated the sea. The bay stretched out wide and even, the yellow sands a slice of lightness amid the dark blue sea and brown rocks. A few houses clustered, then thinned out, then clustered again, on the inland side of the road. The road was just wide enough for two cars to pass, and Charley slowed her speed, doing her best to focus even as the sea beside her made her feel nauseous. An older person with a wide-brimmed hat tended a little garden, while two figures constructed an elaborate sandcastle. Aside from that, the coastline seemed deserted. The sandy beach gave way to rugged rocks as she drove north, seals basking comfortably on the crags.

Twice she had to stop, shaking and nauseous. Twice she took a drink of water, counted to 20, and drove on. It was like the waves were crashing inside her head and salt was burning her eyes. She'd tried asking a doctor about it once, and he'd shrugged and said maybe she was allergic to a coastal plant, prescribed her antihistamines and eye drops. They didn't help. She doubted it was about a plant anyway, but who on earth was allergic to the sea?

Her GPS alerted her that she was getting close to her destination. Her whole head was spinning, and she didn't know how she was going to get through any kind of conversation without sounding like a crank.

As she rounded a corner, a wide bay came into view; the far headland was dark with bush, and what seemed to be the remnants of a stone tower stood right at the top. She passed a couple of boatsheds on the right. To her left, a scattering of small houses – wood painted in whites and pale yellow-browns – were built into the hillside.

At the northern end of the bay, the road turned inland, just ahead of where a small river emptied into the sea. Charley had reached her destination. She found a space by a cluster of houses and what looked like a scarcely-used sports field and pulled her car over. She clambered out and dusted herself down. Something was stuck to her shoe, and she raised her foot and pulled what seemed to be an old receipt off the sole. She chucked it in her car, amongst the food wrappers and assortment of random items that had accumulated in there. It was a fucking mess, just like her life. She slammed the door and locked it, took a pen from her pocket and drew a small circle on her wrist as a reminder, another failing system to try to organise her life.

There wasn't a person in sight. She followed the road back and was pleased to find the address easily, the number 3 in irregular mosaic pieces, like fragments of a smashed plate, inlaid into a wall, blue number on white. Looking up from it she saw a winding, twisting path, with occasional steps cut into it and retaining walls on the uphill sides. The walls were decorated with rocks, shells, and orb-like buoys. As she climbed they were joined by driftwood, nets and seagrass, even skeletons of impossible creatures to make up a vast three-dimensional collage. Charley would have appreciated a handrail as she walked up over the uneven path, but she figured touching the wall wouldn't be a good idea.

As she followed the path up and round she saw the sea, and far out along the extent of the coastline, the occasional boat in the distance. At last, she reached the top – an old cottage with seaweed hanging above the doors, clustered with a couple of smaller buildings to make a sort of semi-courtyard. There was a little flat paved area with a barrel about as high as Charley's hip, and a rudimentary bench seat. She could see beehives set a little further back into the hill, along a narrow foot track, and behind them a small cluster of fruit trees, all with full crops; cherries and apples, and also... were those lemons, this far south? A sign read: *If door is closed please wait here. Be patient.* Charley looked in the barrel. It was full of water, and small creatures swam far below the surface. She couldn't help but feel it ran far deeper than the ground. She took a seat and waited as directed, catching up on her messages with the one bar of reception.

An hour passed. Charley was starting to wish she'd found somewhere to use the bathroom, but in a place as small as this she doubted there were many options, and she'd have preferred her arrival not to be heralded by someone finding her squatted behind a bush. Still, things were getting uncomfortable. Charley paced the little yard and played flash games on her phone. She wondered if patience was not, in fact, a virtue.

About 40 minutes later, she heard noises down the hill, car doors opening and closing, and then slow footsteps. Charley looked but couldn't see anything. A few minutes later though, a child of about ten appeared, pale skin and dark hair with stripes shaved into the sides, his arms loaded with supermarket bags, puffing as he reached the top.

"Thalassa's right behind me," he said. "I'm just the pack horse."

"None of that cheek," said a voice from further back. "A little more respect for your elders would do you a world of good."

Charley stood and dusted herself down, swallowing. This wasn't going to be an easy encounter. Behind the child came the person she assumed was Thalassa – a woman whose long white hair flowed behind her, her face wrinkled and sea-hardened, dressed in a long dress with a knitted shawl buttoned across it. Despite her apparent age, she stood straight, one hand on what appeared to be a driftwood staff that stood taller than she did. The child left the bags and ducked past, running down to the street.

Thalassa looked Charley up and down, appearing not to blink. Charley felt small and scruffy, as if she was still a school kid about to be in trouble for not tucking in her shirt. She felt vulnerable, as if Thalassa were seeing more than just her appearance.

Charley took off her sunglasses and coughed, desperate to break the silence. "Your grandson?" she asked nervously.

"Ha, no! Just one of the locals. You can get them to do all sorts for you. I assume you've come to engage my services?"

"Yes, please. My name's Charley Deacon, and I..."

"Take a seat at the dining table while I get the cold stuff away."

"Thank you. Do you need a hand with anything?"

"Ah no. No. The hill's a little difficult but other than that I'm fully capable."

"Um, is there a toilet I can use please?"

"Of course there's a toilet, I'm old but I don't live in the middle ages. Down the corridor, last door on the right."

At this point, Charley would have been thankful for a long drop, but there was a modern toilet behind the door, and sitting down with the door closed she felt more like she could do this, that the worst was behind her, that she could find Melissa and all would be well again. She emerged through a hallway decorated with seascapes, photos of jellyfish, and a framed copy of that one *New Zealand Seafood* poster that is in every single chip shop.

Thalassa pointed a bony finger at a wooden chair and set a mug down in front of it. "Drink this. It will help your headache."

The tea Thalassa had strained for Charley smelled disgusting; it was thick and grey with hints of green. She sipped at it anyway, trying not to think about the fact she'd never mentioned she had a headache. Surprisingly she did soon feel better; the nausea lifted after only a few sips, and halfway through the contents of the delicate china cup she was feeling almost normal. She supposed she'd have to ask what was in it – it was the only thing that had ever really helped her reactions – but she wasn't sure she wanted to know.

Thalassa took the chair opposite her, with a folder of papers in front of her. "Missing person?" she asked.

"Yes, my sister. Melissa."

Thalassa pulled out some papers from the folder. "Here's my standard contract. You can get a lawyer to look it over if you like, but I doubt you have time to waste on that. So the main points are that you will tell me the truth, and you won't hold me liable for anything. If I don't find your sister you don't pay, if I find her you do, and terrible things will happen to you if you don't give me what I'm owed. Finding her doesn't mean you have to like the circumstances. If I find your sister dead, you still pay. If you find she's been on the meth, or with the wrong crowd, or sleeping with your man, you still pay. If she's about to be caught sneaking pain pills like most doctors seem to be these days, you still pay. Got it?"

Charley nodded. "I don't have a lot of money, but our parents will be able to come up with it..."

"Ah no. No. If you don't have the money, I'm not faffing around going after parents and sugar daddies and fairy godmothers. I'm too old for that. If you don't have the money you pay with time. Seven years of your life."

Charley blinked, trying to process what she'd just heard. "Seven years... you mean I have to work for you?"

"No no no. Indentured servitude is illegal these days. Along with recreational opiates and everything else fun. I mean, what's your life expectancy, maybe 85? 90 if you've got this far? So if I take seven years you still live to say 83, which is a very respectable age, and I live an extra seven. How's that for an arrangement?"

Charley suppressed a giggle. She didn't know if the instinct came from nerves or disbelief. She'd never been asked to agree to the impossible before – the unreasonable, yes, she'd worked in retail for long enough, but not the literally physically impossible. And yet... she was here for the impossible. Nothing about Melissa's disappearance had been normal. She was here for the weird, the impossible... maybe even the magical.

Charley looked into Thalassa's eyes, deep blue like a baby's, and realised she was far older than she looked. It felt like there were whole worlds hidden in those...

Charley forcibly cut off her gaze, drinking the dregs of the suspicious tea. "You'll kill me?"

"It's nothing personal. I don't control the means – heart attack or stroke, most commonly, but it depends. You probably won't see it coming."

Charley felt like her head was spinning. Sacrificing years of her life seemed ridiculous, but the thought of never finding Melissa, never knowing what had happened to her, seemed far more agonising. And as Thalassa had said, she probably would be old by then anyway. And chances are this was a load of nonsense... either it wasn't true, in which case she didn't have anything to worry about – or if magic was real, this could be her only hope of finding Melissa.

Thalassa opened a drawer and pulled out a vial half-full of what looked like water. She wrote Charley's name and the date on a label, affixed it to the glass vial, and removed the lid. It smelled of the sea, more strongly than such a small amount of sea water should.

She held out a needle to Charley. "Prick your fingertip, and then seven drops of blood in there."

Everything in Charley's head was telling her this was ridiculous, that she should run from here, get in her car, and never return to this weird and unsettling place. But she had a sister missing in mysterious circumstances, and someone who knew how to treat the bizarre ailment no doctor had been able to diagnose. She was on the verge of finding out so much that she couldn't just go back now.

She winced as she pricked her finger, but the blood flowed easily. She could have sworn the liquid glowed for a moment after the seventh drop reached it, but then it was nothing more than vaguely murky water.

Charley leaned over to see Thalassa put the vial back in the drawer. Along with what looked like several others.

The second cup of tea was more normal. Still herbal – Charley doubted there was decent coffee or anything round here – but less suspicious in appearance and consistency. Her hand trembled as she raised her cup. She told herself this was just woo anyway, like psychics who can't really speak to spirits but are sometimes helpful because they pick up on clues others miss. It didn't feel like that though. She'd basically just sold her soul.

"Tell me about Melissa," Thalassa said. She held a pen between her thin fingers.

Charley had heard the question so many times over the past couple of days that she rattled off the details easily. "She's 23, blonde, 5 foot 8 or 172 centimetres, what they call athletic build. She's a medical student at Otago, almost finished. She's good at basically everything. She's kind and she never forgets your birthday and..."

"Boyfriends, girlfriends, other partners?"

Charley shook her head. "Never. She's been too focused on school."

Thalassa arched an eyebrow, like she didn't believe a word of it, but continued. "Involvement in crime, gangs, cults..."

Charley shook her head again and realised, embarrassed, she was crying. "Melissa's not like that. She studies. She plays the violin. Her idea of letting go is two wines with her friends over a meal out."

"So, a perfectionist. You sure she's not just stressed?"

"She's always dealt with stress before," Charley said carefully. "And she seemed to be on track to do well. And it's true that people sometimes go missing because of stress, but... they don't tend to leave sea water in their bedrooms, do they?"

"Tell me more."

"So Melissa and I flat together with two others. I do shift work and I'm a bit nocturnal so I was up playing games all night, and Melissa had work early in the morning. Her bedroom opens into the living room, there's no other way out, and I had headphones on but I'd still have seen her. In the morning I got a message from one of her classmates, colleagues, whatever you call them, he wanted to know where she was because it was a really important day for them. So I thought she'd overslept, went to her room, and... there was no sign of her. She left everything behind, her keys, her wallet, her phone. Her car was parked outside. And in her room... everything smelled of the sea. Her chair was mostly damp, and where it had dried you could see little rings of salt round the edges."

"And you knew it was sea water and not just water someone had added salt to because…"

"Well, there were little scraps of seaweed as well. But I got a friend who studies marine science to look at the micro-organisms in the water, and it's consistent with what you find round the Otago coast, right down to the fragments of yellow penguin shell in it. So if it wasn't sea water, someone had gone to a lot of effort to fake it, and why would someone do that when the sea's right there?"

"I see you're a smart one like your sister."

Charley grinned and looked down.

"Quite the opposite actually, but if I've done the right thing here I'm glad."

"Let me ask you: what do you think happened to your sister?"

Charley let out a long breath. "My parents think she's just dealing with some stress and will be back soon."

"Didn't ask about your parents. What do you think?"

Charley played with the cord on her hoodie. "I don't know, but I think, maybe, she's got in over her head with something. She's not… naïve, like, she's good at sorting things out for me, but she's really friendly and tries to help everybody. I think maybe someone asked for her help and she said yes too easily. And she got in trouble."

"Ah." Thalassa wrote down some notes. If there was any magic going on, Charley wasn't seeing it, but she guessed anyone happy to be paid in some mystical transfer of life expectancy must either be the real thing or at least genuinely believe they are.

"Did your sister like to swim?" Thalassa asked, looking up.

"Sure. I mean, she wasn't competitive or anything, but she had fun when we went to the beach, and always used to spend summers in the water when we were kids. I'm not sure she's had much time for that lately, but I expect she'd still enjoy it."

Thalassa scribbled a bit more, appeared to think for a moment, and then closed up the notebook. She rested her hands on it, as though pondering what to do next.

"I can't search for your sister today," she said eventually. "I'm not young, you'll be surprised to learn, and the trip up to town to get groceries takes more of my energy than it should, but tomorrow. Talk to Gordon if you need somewhere to stay."

Charley sucked on her lower lip, forcing herself not to panic. She wanted to be searching all night. She wanted to do whatever it took. But she knew she couldn't push this one and nodded, numbly.

"Gordon?" she asked, realising too late that she hadn't even thought this far ahead, had only got as far as *get to the old woman who is possibly a witch and lives on a clifftop*. Once again, she was disorganised. She supposed she could sleep in her car, but if there was a better option...

"Gordon, the guy who runs the holiday park, he'll sort out a cabin or something. Good rate now, before the season hits. I'd say don't let him con you but he's not the sort – too nice, in my estimation. Come and see me again at nine. Don't be late."

Charley felt the woman's eyes on her the whole way down the steep narrow path. She spat on her wrist to rub the mark off, the one she made to reassure herself that yes, she had locked the car, and yes she had her keys with her so if she lost them she could at least trace back to that point. She drove down to the first turnoff on the left and along the short road to the holiday park. Behind her, the river was trickling down to the sea, and the evening waves were cracking onto the rocks.

Charley's dinner was teriyaki chicken noodles selected from the microwaveable meal options that the holiday park sold, followed by a Moro bar. It wasn't as bad as she'd feared. The kitchen wasn't terrible either, especially as she had virtually no one to share it with, and she'd paid for the loan of a plate, cup, and cutlery set. Therese, who was Gordon's wife and ran the place with him, had given her an extra blanket. She had her laptop and, though the Wi-Fi wasn't good enough for streaming, she had some TV saved to her hard drive.

It could all have been worse.

Except for the very reason she was here, it all felt like a welcome break. Not a holiday exactly – everything holiday-like about this place depended on the weather, and it was still the erratic, windy, drizzly days of spring – but a reset from the rest of her life. A reminder that she might be a failure, but she *could* survive.

Charley rinsed out her plate and cutlery and dropped them in the cabin. In theory, she could have cabin mates at any time – there was space for five more across the three bunk beds – but Gordon had basically hinted he wouldn't put anyone in with her unless it got suddenly busy. He only charged her for a shared room. Thalassa had said he was too nice.

Then she headed out of the holiday park, swore, returned to lock her cabin, and headed out again. *She would forget her head if it wasn't screwed on*, her grandmother always said. She turned up the road, towards the bridge. There were more signs of life in the settlement in the dying light – televisions flickered through windows, and voices and the scent of tobacco smoke drifted from nowhere in particular. Over on the riverbank, a group of teens were perched with a bottle of something and plastic cups, their laughter audible above the rush of water. They looked at Charley with curiosity, but she nodded at them and continued along her way. There was no footpath over the bridge, and even though there was no sign of traffic Charley kept uneasily to the edge.

Her phone buzzed in her pocket and she checked her messages: no sign of Melissa. Their flatmate Rae said there was a parcel for her, it was on her bed, and wanted to know if she'd found anything. Liam asked if she wanted them to cover her shift at the shop. She'd forgotten all about it, texted back frantically.

She would say she'd lost track of time since she'd come here, but the truth is she'd always been like that.

"You okay?"

In the time she had been standing there, almost all the daylight had disappeared from the settlement. Charley looked up to see a face vaguely lit by the glow of her cell phone, pale skin, eyes framed by round, thin-rimmed glasses. Panicking, briefly, wondering if she looked wrong in some way, and then realising the woman was probably only asking if she was okay because she was a person new to town standing around at night in a T-shirt.

"Oh yeah, sorry, I'm fine. Just taking a walk before I sleep."

The woman looked as if she was weighing up her thoughts. "You don't live here and it's too early for summer visitors, so I'm guessing either you have a relative here or you're here for…" and here she gestured to Thalassa's clifftop house. "Less natural reasons."

Charley felt uneasy. "My sister's gone missing. Someone told me she could find her. I'm not usually into that stuff but I'm desperate."

"I'm sorry. I'm True, by the way."

"Charley."

"Well, Charley. I hope you find her. Just… be careful."

Charley wanted to ask her what she should be careful of, but the woman was already walking confidently back across the bridge, back straight, head held high. Her emerald green duffel coat that was perfectly fitted around her hips looked almost black in the dying light. Her hair was behind her in a thick plait.

Probably of giving away seven years of her life. For all the bad decisions her parents had predicted her making, that must have been one they'd failed to see coming. Charley's gaze lingered on the young woman's figure until she was almost out of sight. She put away her phone and looked down the river out to sea. She'd never imagined being able to be near the sea like this, to have her head so clear, to not have her whole body reacting. There was discomfort and a little queasiness, for sure, but she was handling it better than she could have imagined.

Back on the campground side of the bridge, a man was good-naturedly shepherding his wayward teen back home. The scent of rum hung in the air. Charley turned on her phone torch to help keep her footing. A couple of older people – permanent residents of the holiday park, she suspected – greeted her as she passed and she replied in turn, making her way to the cabin.

Chapter Two

Morning flickered through the flimsy curtain. Charley checked her phone, plugged into the charger. She'd forgotten to include trousers in the clothes she'd flung in the back of her car before she left, but her jeans would last another day and mercifully she had clean underwear at least. She had plenty of time – she could take a walk by the Aora River, explore the rest of the settlement, catch up on some messages.

And yet somehow, inexplicably, by the time she was ready to go it was already after nine. Shit. How had it been an hour? How could it take anyone this long?

Charley crammed the cereal bar that came in the "breakfast pack" she'd bought from Gordon – the holiday park turned out to be the only place in Inver Aora that sold food – into her mouth and hurried down the road and up the steep pathway to Thalassa's house. The sun was piercing and uncomfortable but she didn't have time to go back for her sunglasses. She tried to ignore the growing nausea, the discomfort she felt with the sea just round the corner. As she walked she looked in her bag for a hair tie or something to tame her mass of unbrushed hair, but if she had any of them there was no finding them amid the accumulation of debris that was lodged in there. The only saving grace was that she'd showered before she went to sleep, but she still felt dirty and unkempt, a bad representative of her family.

The glass doors to the dining room were open when she reached the top of the pathway, and Thalassa was sitting at the table, dressed in a teal tunic and loose dark trousers, with a necklace of sea glass. Her hair, in contrast to Charley's, was up in a tidy bun.

"I'm so sorry I'm late, I..."

"Your tea is going cold," Thalassa said, pointing to it.

Charley nodded with relief. She could cope – she wasn't feeling as bad as when she'd first arrived – but it was a relief not to have to. "Sorry," she said again, and sat down, sipping the tea which was at least still warm, if not hot. She caught a brief scent of jasmine in it. She swallowed a mouthful trying not to taste it.

"Here's something for you," Thalassa said, handing over a slip of paper. On it was scrawled the name of a doctor, followed by a phone number.

"This is someone who can help find my sister?" Charley asked, looking up.

"Dr Pedrick is a very good psychiatrist of my acquaintance. I suggest you make an appointment. He has a waiting list, but if you tell him I sent you he'll find a spot for you. He'll let you pay off the cost, as well. He only accepts dollars, not time."

"A psych... you think I'm crazy? You think I'm making all this up?" Charley shot to her feet, her face burning, tears welling. She'd gone to so much effort and now she was just being dismissed.

Thalassa rolled her eyes. "Sit down and calm down. I don't think you're crazy. I don't even think you're mentally ill, though there's no shame in that. I'm suggesting you call him because you've shown at least five classic signs of attention deficit hyperactivity disorder, and I think it's obscuring what else is going on in your brain. You're exhausted, just trying to deal with the effects of that. I may be wrong. But if something is going on for you, the sooner you get a handle on that the sooner we can get to the other stuff."

"The other... attention..."

"Attention deficit disorder. ADD or ADHD, they change the names with the fashion and I can't keep up with it. Anyway, you forget things. You can't focus or you focus too much and can't snap out of it. You don't have a good sense of time. You're always late. Sound familiar?"

Charley felt suddenly cold, wanting a blanket, wanting Melissa, wanting to be anywhere but here. "And they can treat it?"

"There are meds that help. Or ways of dealing with it. If it is that, and I'd place money on it. If anyone gambled with me. Which they don't. Sensible of them. Anyway, I'm not promising. I'm not a doctor, I'm just very old. But I reckon he can help you one way or another. Might be able to help you focus enough to finish a course of study..."

"I never mentioned..."

"You came to see someone who's widely referred to as a witch because there was something weird and possibly supernatural about your sister's disappearance. You can't do that and then complain that there are certain things I can do that don't make rational sense to you. Really? If you're freaked out I know things about you that you didn't explicitly say then we probably need to stop the whole process, because things are about to get very weird for you."

"No... I... just lots to take in," Charley stammered. "You said other stuff going on, aside from the attention disorder..."

Thalassa turned away. "We're already running late. We'd better hurry if you want to find your sister. You got a photo of her?"

Charley started scrolling through her phone.

"No, child, a photo, on paper, unless you want to sacrifice your phone to the eternal depths."

The idea seemed momentarily tempting. It was so quiet out here; even on a thin bunkbed mattress in a cold cabin, Charley had slept better than she had in months. But, feeling her face start to redden, she unfolded a small stash of MISSING posters, cast aside the outer one because it had something suspicious stuck to it, and passed the second over to Thalassa.

She stared at Melissa's face on the remaining stack of posters for a few moments, one of a series of portrait shots their parents had organised a couple of years ago. Melissa's hair, though wavy, was neat in a bob, and her smile was calm and professional. She probably wasn't the sort of person who would stand out to most people. If she wanted to go missing she could change her appearance easily and be hard to recognise. But why would Melissa want to go missing? If she needed a break from exams, if she didn't want to study medicine anymore, she'd at least tell Charley. She must have known Charley would keep her secrets – as she'd kept plenty of Charley's over the years.

No, something much more than that was very, very wrong.

"We need to go down to the beach for this," Thalassa said. "Bring that bag there with you please."

The bag felt like it was full of rocks, but Charley knew better than to complain, swinging it over her shoulder and following Thalassa down the path. There was nothing that separated the coastal road from the beach; tarmac gave way to uneven rocks and then a wide expanse of sand. Charley spread out her free arm to help her balance as they climbed down, seeing the usefulness of Thalassa's staff.

The day was grey but dry, the sand more a dusty pale brown than golden. The waves seemed tipped with an unpleasant-smelling foam, and seaweed was smeared on the rocks. Over in the distance, Charley could see some figures – an adult and two children – walking over the rocks, and a single car went past, but otherwise, there was little sign of life. Thalassa nodded to Charley who, relieved, placed the bag on the sand.

Thalassa moved with the staff, creating vast lines in the sand, great sweeping motions that read almost like a dance to Charley. One circle with a symbol in it, like an ancient letter, and then another.

"The good thing is that water holds a memory of magic that has been worked in or on it. And that thing with the sea water in your sister's room – I don't quite know what went on, but I'm confident it wasn't some joker dragging a couple of buckets up the path."

"Memory like homeopathy?" asked Charley, squinting in the daylight. She instantly panicked that she'd said the wrong thing.

"So, interestingly, the water memory isn't the most dubious part of homeopathy. That's solid, if you have a magic worker be part of it, which most of these charlatans don't. The like-cures-like thing is much more suspicious – arguable for a minority of conditions, but hardly a universal principle. Open the bag."

The bag was, as it turned out, full of rocks. They were more blue than grey, and well-rounded by the sea. Charley picked one out. It seemed to hum in her hand, warm to the touch. Thalassa took the picture of Melissa and put it in the middle of one of the sigils, muttering something under her breath that Charley couldn't hear. Oddly, despite the coastal winds and the crashing waves just beyond them, the picture didn't blow away, just fluttered there slightly, Melissa's face in the middle of this godforsaken coastline. When she was finally found, Charley reckoned Melissa would find this funny.

"Rock goes in the middle of that one, then get out," Thalassa instructed. Charley stepped gingerly forward, into the wind, wondering if this was all ridiculous. She felt almost like she was being pranked.

Still, she was here now. There was a small circle in the centre of the sigil and she crouched down and placed the stone in there.

Then everything lit up, rushing round the sigil, glowing golden. Charley stood and turned round in wonder. Everything seemed so much bigger, so much clearer than before; the river mouth, the houses clinging to the hillside, and the sea, the wide-open sea...

"Get out now, Charley."

The voice seemed to come from far away. Everything was glowing and beautiful and wonderous, there were so many more layers to everything than Charley had ever realised – the crash of the waves seems to have different notes to it, the squawk of a seagull overhead its own kind of music, complete and beautiful. Charley felt like she could understand the universe, all the world's waters, deeply connected.

The glow shot up into flames, higher than Charley's head. She thought to herself she should be scared, but she wasn't. She walked over to the edge and looked at the flames. They didn't feel hot. Through them, she could see the world outside, a little distorted but still there.

"Get out. Get out now."

Charley couldn't explain, then or later, how she knew she could walk through the flames, but she did so and ended up untouched. Either they were a cooler temperature than real fire, or she was re-sistant, but either way, she barely felt them. And then she was on the beach, just an ordinary-looking beach, and then the water came rushing in, not as one tide but as purposeful channels, widening each mark of the sigil and filling it with water. She sat down backwards, her hands propping her up on the damp sand. Thalassa stood between the circles, her loose clothes billowing in the wind, her staff held firm.

Charley found herself shaking. She'd known, of course, that some-thing was going on with Thalassa, something that couldn't quite be explained. But she'd expected, like, tarot cards, or psychic readings. Not grand, showy, absolutely unambiguous magic.

She grasped her legs with her hands to try to keep them still, her heart rate pounding. So magic *was* real after all.

No one from Inver Aora seemed to be watching. Had Thalassa somehow cast a spell to stop them from seeing, or were they just so used to weird magic happening nearby that it didn't even register for them?

Then the water rushed out as quickly as it had come in, leaving everything looking surprisingly normal. The sand felt damp and uncomfortable, and the air smelled of seaweed on the edge of rotting. Charley scrambled to her feet, realising she felt sore. The poster fluttered through the air and caught on a gust of wind, and Thalassa, seemingly without effort, reached up and caught it. She looked at it, as if for the first time, and nodded as if she found the contents interesting. Then she shoved it into a pocket and walked over to the stone, which she picked up and hurled into the sea with much more strength than Charley would have thought she'd be able to muster. She yelled something as she did, but Charley couldn't make out any of the words against the increasing roar of the sea.

"You're very lucky you didn't ruin it all with your silly disobedience," Thalassa said, walking past Charley and up to the road. Her expression was more thoughtful than angry. "Grab the bag and head back."

She made me bring the whole bag when we were just using one stone, Charley thought, her face burning with shame as well as anger as she made her way up the stairs. Thalassa turned and looked at her momentarily, but said nothing. Charley wasn't even sure how to tell if she was reading her mind. But she supposed she had to be careful irrespective. She was curious about Thalassa and wanted to know more about what she did, but her goal was to find her sister. She had to keep her distance.

Thalassa held the poster in her hand.

"Let's look at this over some lunch, shall we," she said, her voice softer than it had been but still with an edge of annoyance about Charley's behaviour. "You'll want to charge your phone as well."

Charley frowned – she was sure she'd charged it overnight but when she pulled it out of her pocket it was dead. Thankfully she had a cable with her and Thalassa found her a USB-to-wall converter.

When Thalassa brought the food out, Charley suddenly realised she was hungry. The whole thing, impossibly, had taken several hours. She gratefully accepted the vegetable soup and crusty bread she was offered, the plate of Tim Tams laid out for afterwards. It was odd, she supposed, to think of a witch or magician or whatever Thalassa was going to the supermarket and buying Tim Tams, but she lived in the real world, even if this settlement didn't always feel like it.

As Charley mopped up soup with bread, Thalassa spread out the poster. Charley leaned to look carefully at it. There was Melissa, but the image was distorted – her hair was messier, her face pale, her eyes exhausted. Charley gasped, realising that this wasn't just the effect of water damage to the paper – this was a picture of Melissa as she was now. Wherever she was.

"So she's alive?" Charley asked.

"Looks that way to me," was Thalassa's response. She could at least *try* to sound interested.

But Charley let herself relax, just a little bit. Melissa was alive and they were making progress in finding her.

Along the edges of the paper were unfamiliar glyphs – Charley thought they might be Viking runes, or maybe sigils like Thalassa had used on the beach. Either way, they were totally opaque to her. All the words that had been on the paper were gone. It had been completely transformed.

"They're just a system of symbols," explained Thalassa. "They're not from anything else, they're a form I've created and have pushed meaning into over the years. I'm going to need a bit of time to interpret them. But there's something about finding what others cannot here, and this bit is about fear..." She outlined the symbols with her finger as she spoke.

"Us finding her?" Charley asked. "Or Melissa found something?"

"As I said, I need time to interpret. It's going to be a long night for me, long and tedious, so be thankful."

"Yes. Yes of course. I am."

"I'll see you here at eight-thirty."

Charley wanted to ask why Thalassa had included her in the ritual. It didn't make sense for it to be as simple as needing her to carry bags of rocks, and it didn't seem like the magic required Charley's presence, or anyone but Thalassa's, really. But this was not the time for asking questions. This was the time for not poking the bear, and giving Thalassa space to work what Charley hoped would be a miracle. She was allowing herself to hope her sister would be found safe.

Back in her cabin, Charley looked up ADHD on her phone. It was, she learned, divided into three types. As she read the symptoms of the second she felt like something plummeted, very suddenly, inside her chest and down to her stomach. It was like reading not just a portrait of herself, but a list of all the things she'd tried so hard not to be, that she'd tried to disguise. She felt her cheeks burning. She knew it was just a list about no one in particular, but she felt like it was written by someone who knew her way better than she was comfortable with anyone doing.

Sighing, she put on her shoes, reminded herself to lock the door after her, and headed out. Almost to the entrance of the holiday park and she realised she had not, in fact, locked the door and she stopped, wanting to cry or scream. How? How was she always like this? She had literally thought about remembering to lock the door just before she failed to do it. This could be an ADHD sign, but it felt more like a personal failing than a disorder.

The door locked – and actually locked, this time – Charley walked down to the sea, even though the nausea was starting to grow again and every muscle ached. They had gotten so close to doing something, and now she just had to wait. It just wasn't in her bones to do nothing, to be patient, and yet she had to force herself to be.

Charley looked at the waves. She didn't understand why the sea had such a strong effect on her – she wasn't scared of water or drowning, had always been fine beside a river. Someone had suggested it was a form of agoraphobia, that it was the vastness and emptiness of the ocean that set her off, and while it was the most sensible theory she'd come across in a heap of not-very-sensible ones, it still didn't feel quite right. The whole thing seemed deeper and more automatic, more physiological than psychological.

The sigils Thalassa had drawn on the beach had disappeared, disappeared more thoroughly than an incoming tide should have managed. She supposed it wasn't worth wondering how. All she knew was that magic was real, and not in a vague sense that could be explained by just being somewhat more attuned to the world, but actual, dramatic, against the laws of physics magic.

Which also meant she really had given up seven years of her life.

The sand was mostly smooth, sometimes with little ridges pushed up by the water, compacted damp. Perhaps in summer this had a different feel, but now, even with early summer just around the corner, it felt wild and hostile. She pushed herself to stay. Pushed herself to listen to the rhythm of the waves. But there was so much there, it seemed so loud inside her head that she quickly became overwhelmed and nauseous, and her head hurt.

The ocean simply wasn't the place for her, even on a quiet day. And yet she forced herself to stay a little this time, as if she could make sense of it, as if she could understand something about the desperately weird situation her whole life had been plunged into. But deep down, she suspected that was far too much to hope for.

Once she'd looked at a map and found the places furthest from the sea, dreamed about starting a new life in Cairo or Moscow or Chicago. *You could still do that*, she told herself. *You're still young. You've only failed a bit of your life, not the whole thing.*

Soon, she hoped, she'd be able to run away, even if only as far as back to Dunedin, which had a port but you could easily stay away from that side of it. Her sister would be safe, and she'd be away from her parents, and even if she failed out of polytech, even if she ended up working retail forever, she'd never ever have to go back to the sea again.

Charley turned back and clambered over the rocks to the road. The settlement was quiet. She looked up at the headland, the run-down tower silhouetted against the sky in the dying light. An old lighthouse, perhaps, rendered useless in these days of radar and satellite navigation. It was hard to tell from here, but the seed of curiosity had been planted and she walked down the river and across the bridge to the foot of the headland.

She found the path up through the bush without too much trouble, letting the torch on her phone guide her.

The tower came in and out of view as she made her way up the winding path. She heard the scrabble of small animals in the dusk, the call of a ruru, other birdsong she couldn't identify. The hill was steep but the path reasonably defined, and she pushed on, letting her mind wander.

She didn't notice she wasn't alone until the other woman almost bumped into her. She blinked, forcing herself to stop. It was True, the local woman she'd met on the bridge. She kept walking, turning to one side to edge past Charley but otherwise barely acknowledging her presence.

Charley swallowed.

"Hi. Uh."

True spun round on one foot.

"Yes?" she replied sharply. "You need something?"

"No, I, uh. I just came for a walk. I didn't mean to bother you."

"Okay. Well. How about you take your walks alone and I'll do the same."

True turned away and strode quickly down the path and disappeared into the bush before Charley could think what to do or say.

Chapter Three

C harley woke up feeling ill. The nausea was back, and it was as if something was grinding in her head. She kept replaying True's annoyance with her, her cheeks burning with embarrassment. Somehow she managed to shower, pull on jeans – she'd need to do laundry tonight – and a thin hoodie, run a brush through her hair, and make it up the hill 15 minutes late. Shit. Thalassa wouldn't be happy.

The glass doors to the dining room were standing open. There was no sign of Thalassa but a cup of the murky grey-green tea was waiting for her. Charley drank it gratefully, trying to ignore the taste, not questioning how Thalassa knew she'd needed it. Her head started to clear almost immediately.

"We'll be starting at nine," Thalassa called out from another room. "Amuse yourself until then."

"I thought you said..."

"Got you here on time, though didn't it." Charley waited for the barbs, the *amazing what you can do if you try*, but none followed. The comment was of sheer practicality, not of triumph. She fiddled with a spare hair tie while she waited. It wasn't the first time someone had used precisely that tactic on Charley, but it was normally about teaching her a lesson, of proving something. Not just a simple matter of being able to start on time. The room smelled of aromatic wood, and when Charley looked around a little more, she saw signs that Thalassa had been working on what she supposed was some kind of ritual last night. There were small saucers, for want of a better word, laid out in what seemed to be a pattern, and some of them contained ashes or little heaps of sugar or salt. Salt made entirely more sense.

Charley looked at her phone. Her parents were about to fly to Dunedin and wanted to know where she was. Did they now have two daughters missing, they asked; was she looking for attention or had she really decided to take a holiday in a time of crisis? Charley posted one reply: *I'm looking for Melissa*, and then she turned her phone off. Her heart rate sped up. She couldn't believe she'd actually done it – she'd never cut them off like that before.

Thalassa appeared in the doorway carrying papers and a handful of small stones, some looking like smaller versions of the ones Charley had had to carry down to the beach – and then back up again. But no use dwelling on that now. Thalassa sat down opposite, and Charley listened to what she had to say.

"Here's what I'm confident we know about your sister. It's connected to the sea. We know she's still alive – or at least she was yesterday, and there's nothing to suggest imminent danger. And she's not able to return home on her own. Whether that means she's being held against her will or she's trapped somewhere, or even that she's lost or has memory issues, I can't tell you, but she hasn't chosen to take a break because of exam stress, I'll give you that."

"Thanks," Charley said. "It, uh. It means a lot to know that she's still safe."

"There's an ambiguous symbol. It could mean protecting or guarding. It suggests that someone – and you understand that when I say someone I don't necessarily mean a human – might be with her, but if they're protecting her from something, or if they're standing guard to stop her escaping, I can't say right now."

Charley nodded numbly. She knew any information was good to have, but she didn't quite know what to make of the last bit. *Not necessarily human.* What could that mean?

She wanted to message her parents to say Melissa was safe, or at least alive, but decided against it. It was selfish, but as soon as they knew she was onto something they would descend all guns blazing, and she couldn't imagine that going well, knew that it might end up sabotaging their best hope. And that's if they even believed her – it wasn't like she exactly had proof. No. Her phone stayed in her pocket. They could resolve all this when Melissa was found – hopefully – or at least they'd be so pleased to see Melissa that they'd forget their latest issues with Charley.

She could hope.

Never mind. She did need to keep them updated on anything major as they searched for Melissa but that wasn't going to last forever. Once they found Melissa – and Charley was still talking as if finding her was a certainty, because it was – then the decision was hers again. She might not be successful by their metrics, but she was an adult, an adult who hadn't accepted money from them in a long time. She could set boundaries of her own, and if they didn't stick to them then it was their loss, not hers.

At least that was theoretically the case. She wasn't sure how well she'd be able to hold up in practice.

Thalassa pointed at another piece of paper. "And these three symbols here, she's surrounded by water, and she's there because of her work."

"Work like at the hospital?"

"That would be my guess. Though I suppose it could expand to any labour expended, even housework, but yes, the hospital is most likely."

"And by surrounded by water, would that be a boat? Or could it mean an island?"

"It could," Thalassa said, her tone half mysterious and half resigned. "And then there's this circle. I really shouldn't have used a circle at all when I set up this system. Because circles can mean anything. Eternity. Connections. Symmetry. The snake that eats its own tail. The letter O. The number zero. I tried to get a clearer read on it, but it came to nothing. The only thing that came up was the number eight. So I was thinking maybe pieces of eight..."

"Like the parrots say?"

"Yes. The Spanish dollar, the first international currency in some ways. You know, a circle like a coin. I doubt it's literal, I wouldn't expect any Spanish dollars around here – they had their heyday hundreds of years ago. But it might mean finances. You say your sister wasn't in any financial trouble?"

Charley shook her head. "I mean she was a student, she was broke, but we all are. Our parents were paying her rent, so she was better off than some. She didn't gamble or anything like that."

"Not that you'd necessarily know."

Charley resisted the urge to tell the old woman where to shove her thoughts. In theory, she supposed, she was right; people with addictions often didn't tell their families about them. But she knew Melissa in a way no one else could.

Leaving Thalassa to make some calls, Charley headed back down the hill to the holiday park. Gordon was in the office, so Charley stopped to pick up another microwaveable meal, selecting what was generously called ravioli in some kind of shelf-stable three-cheese sauce. She noted none of the three cheeses were specified. If she ended up staying much longer she was going to have to make the journey to the nearest town and pick up a few things.

"Anything else?" Gordon asked. After a moment's thought, Charley chose a chocolate bar and another breakfast pack. Nothing was getting solved tonight, that had been made clear.

She looked up to see Gordon frowning at her. "Uh. Everything okay?" she asked.

"Sorry. Yes. You haven't been in for any other food or anything today, have you? Or taken any of the water bottles? It's not a big deal as long as you settle it, I just want to know."

Charley shook her head. "I haven't taken water bottles at all. And I spoke to you or Therese about the food. Why, is something missing?"

"I probably just miscounted, but it feels like we have less than we should. It'll just be a stocktake issue, not to worry. Anyway, if we're not here, I don't mind if you grab something, just leave a note by the EFTPOS terminal or let us know the next time you see us."

"I will," Charley said, raising her hand to him as she left. In truth, a miscount of bags of chippies was the least of her concerns right now, and she didn't think she could care about it if she tried.

The weather was pleasant. Charley grabbed her laptop and took it to one of the picnic benches along with her lunch, hot-spotting data from her phone, trying to catch up on some emails, asking what she could do about her course of study – was a late withdrawal an option given the special circumstances or was a failing grade inevitable? Everything had fallen by the wayside – her organisational systems, which never seemed to work how they should, had collapsed entirely, and it felt like the rest of her life had gone with them.

She tried not to think about True, but it was hard not to. Rejection – any kind of rejection – had always hit her hard. Silly and overemotional, her parents had called it, and in this particular respect, they'd been right. She'd burst into tears when she'd asked about a brand of cereal and it wasn't in stock, refused to go to the library for over a year after they told her they didn't have the book she was looking for. She knew it wasn't personal, but it set off something in her head. When it did seem motivated by personal distaste for her... well Charley was on the edge of shaking and crying, even though she knew she had far more important things to be worrying about. She hadn't even been able to carry on up to the top of the headland after last night's encounter; it had been all she could do to get herself back to the relative privacy of the cabin.

Her thoughts were interrupted by her phone ringing. She looked at it suspiciously, but this was a time when she did really need to answer calls. It was a classmate of Melissa's, someone Charley had wanted to talk to about the experiments she'd heard they were doing.

"We'd often sign up for these experiments," they said. "We were encouraged to do it in first year and it felt like a worthy thing to do. Melissa did a bunch of them, even though she didn't really have the time."

"What, they were testing experimental drugs?" Charley grimaced.

"No, the process for those is way more involved. This was just simple stuff, like remembering things when they played different music. Or like, there's this thing called an unconscious bias test, which is basically you rate different faces and it tells you how racist you are without thinking about it. So we'd do that after watching different video clips so they could see if they reinforced stereotypes. I think. Or

I did one last year where you wore a pedometer for two weeks and one week they sent you motivational texts and the next week they didn't. Not risky stuff at all. More like, who has time for that in fifth-year med?"

Charley felt similarly wary. Admittedly Melissa liked to help people, liked to be praised. But it hardly seemed the best use of her time. She wasn't sure where to take it from here – was there a way of getting hold of the names of those running the experiments and see if they knew anything? Between herself and Thalassa they were already in touch with most of the people Melissa had been in contact with.

That evening, back in the cabin, Charley looked up the doctor whose details Thalassa had given her. He was part of a group of specialists with a practice in Dunedin. It seemed a world away. She wrote an email, mentioning Thalassa's name, thanking them in advance for their help. She wondered what on Earth she was doing, and if this would make things easier or harder in the long run.

After she'd sent it she lay back on her bunk for a good 20 minutes, not doing anything, almost afraid to breathe, as if she had exerted herself a great deal rather than sent a short and mostly simple email.

The reply, oddly, came back within the hour. Charley was not used to doctors being responsive, but she supposed they had to be if you were the one paying them, or maybe it was just Thalassa's influence. Of course, he would be happy to see her, conveniently there'd been a cancellation in three weeks. There was a description of the assessment process, a fee that seemed unimaginable to Charley and yet she knew she was somehow going to end up paying, and some forms to be filled in in advance by Charley and another one to be completed "ideally by your parents, or if not someone else who knew you as a child".

Shit. She did not want to hear what her parents thought of her as a child, nor did she want to tell them about this. They'd tell her it was just an excuse for being lazy. She couldn't face it. Just when she'd thought she was getting somewhere.

Who else had known her as a child? Not many people she was still in touch with. Except for Melissa. Melissa had known her as a child.

But Melissa wasn't here.

Everything erupted in Charley's brain in a blaze of betrayal and anger and grief. Rage and guilt at feeling betrayed all surged in her all at once.

She flung open the door and walked barefoot into the night. The gravel on the path through the holiday park hurt the soles of her feet but she didn't care. The only lights were those in windows, and one car reversing into a driveway; this place was too small for streetlights. It wasn't like there was anywhere to go, so Charley made the only real choice she had, the only thing she really knew: she was sick of the sea, sick to death of it, and didn't want to go anywhere near there again.

So she went inland, up the road by the river that rapidly became single track and gravel, her footsteps heavy and crunching that gravel beneath her.

"Hey, Charley!"

She kept walking. Whoever it was and whatever they wanted, she didn't want to deal with them right now. Hopefully, they'd leave her alone if she just ignored them.

No such luck. The sound of faster footsteps now, running over gravel.

"Charley! The river's faster than it looks and it's night, please don't."

It was True, her thick hair loose. Charley turned away from her, unable to stop the flood of tears, and True took her arm and navigated her to a concrete block she could sit down on, the river rushing past behind them. The stars were brighter than Charley had ever seen them before, the sky loud with the full Milky Way, away from the light pollution of the cities.

"I thought you wanted to take your walks alone," she said bitterly.

"No. I'm sorry. I was rude to you last night. It's just my evening walks are the only headspace I get on my own, away from the kids, and... I really needed it yesterday."

"I'm sorry, I should have been more aware someone else might be up there. I just wanted to look at the lighthouse."

"It's okay. Has Thalassa caused you trouble? Because I've always been really curious about what would happen if someone tried to fight her, and I'm happy to give it a go."

Charley laughed despite herself, and it turned into an ugly snort. "Oh god. I'm sorry." She felt the tears coming again, for no particular reason.

"You're okay. You're okay." True handed her a tissue. Charley turned away to blow her nose and then everything started tumbling out, the whole story: her sister, her parents, and now Thalassa wanting her to see this *head doctor*. It felt like she couldn't stop until she'd been through everything, and once it was all out she paused, almost stunned.

"I'm sorry. That was too much, you didn't need to know all that."

"It's okay. You know most missing people turn up safe, yeah?"

"I know, but it's really not like Melissa at all." Charley choked down a sob and blew her nose again. "I, uh. I like your coat."

It was an honest compliment. Charley wouldn't have been able to pull off wearing something like that, but with True's thick hair and the curves of her body, it was perfect.

"Clumsy change of subject, but thank you. My mother got it for me in Europe somewhere. She travels a lot."

Charley swallowed, on the edge of a difficult question. "You told me to be careful. What did you mean by that?'

True breathed deeply. "Do you notice how the nights bleed into one? You'd only planned to be here a day, right? And now you've been here a few days and it seems okay. And even though the reason that brought you here was urgent, you're finding everything's sort of taking its time and you feel strangely okay with that?"

Charley had, in fact, been on the edge of noticing that, as if something was continually slipping just out of reach. It wouldn't be something she could really do anything about anyway. Hell, she'd have agreed to an awful lot more than she had in exchange for finding Melissa. She gave a non-committal nod and let True continue what she was saying.

"I'm not saying she's intentionally cast a spell on you or even that there's magic involved rather than it being psychological. Maybe it's something in the land. Who knows? But there's definitely something in it, isn't there? Do you have a cat or anything? I'd make sure someone's feeding it if I were you."

Charley nodded, oddly wishing she did have a cat or something. "Is she..." Charley scratched at her head. "I mean, do people round here like her?"

"We respect our elders. Doesn't really make a difference if we like them or not. But sure, I get on okay with her, though I wouldn't trust her as far as I could throw a stone, personally. But if you're asking if we're some creepy town that's in a cult with the old woman at the helm, then the answer is no. She's just always been here. Longer than any of us can remember. I honestly don't have all that much to do with her. Now I have children of my own I've graduated from being enlisted to carry her groceries."

Charley smiled faintly, remembering the kid bringing the groceries up when she first met Thalassa.

"Ah," True said. "I take it you've already seen that system at work, then. Well, if it works for her. But I think you should probably head back. It's dangerous up here – no, not witchcraft, just the river and how thick the bush is. It's easy to get lost or put your foot off a cliff, and it gets cold out, even in spring."

Charley nodded, wiping away the rest of her tears, and let True escort her to the entrance to the holiday park, embarrassed and yet somewhat calmed, mumbling her appreciation. It was such a relief to find kindness here, even if it was tinged with such an air of the mysterious.

Chapter Four

The next morning, Charley made her way up to Thalassa's house. A couple of stray bees circled her head, presumably from the hives at the back, and she watched them suspiciously. The walk was more difficult than usual and she had to pause part way. She'd woken up feverish and uncomfortable from vivid dreams; endless visions of fish swimming backwards and forwards until it made her dizzy.

Thalassa opened the door and Charley sat on the closest chair and started to unload.

"I've been talking to people about Melissa. My flatmate studies with her, he basically confirmed what I knew. And I talked to another student who said Melissa was always really keen to help and be a subject in experiments, but none of them sounded like a big deal. They're going to try to work out what she was most recently involved in and get back to me."

"Hmm. Grab some paper and work out her last couple of shifts, who she was with, that sort of thing. Note down who you speak to."

Charley drank her morning tea, in what was close to becoming a tradition. She pieced together, as much as she could, where her sister had been working and who with, texting back and forth with her flatmate and a couple of other friends of Melissa she was in contact with. After she was done, Thalassa said she'd do some follow-up that afternoon.

Charley paused as she gathered her things to leave. "There's another thing," she said hesitantly. "And I don't know if it could be relevant to anything or not, but I had these weirdly vivid dreams of fish last night."

"Fish? What type of fish?"

"I don't know... I don't know much about them, but little fish like you'd get in a tank. Maybe tropical rather than goldfish, I'm not sure."

"Not something on the poster, then?"

Charley got up and checked the poster in the hallway. She'd grown up with that poster, like almost every New Zealand child, but never imagined she'd be consulting it as part of a missing persons case. It seemed that if there was a god he was one hell of a prankster.

"None of these," she said as she returned. "They're all very grey. These are brighter."

"Hmm. Do you think you can find me a picture? Or at least draw them if you can't. Maybe pay Lawson a visit – Gordon will point you in the direction of his house – he can identify most kinds of sea creatures. It's probably just a dream, but best to be sure. In the meantime, I think continuing to investigate the work lead is the best option. By the way, your sister didn't wear anything made of silk, did she?"

Charley narrowed her eyes. "Maybe. I mean, our parents bought her nice things. To wear to, like, formal events and stuff, but I wouldn't know what they were made of." Charley forced away all the memories that were coming up, all the comments about how Melissa showed off clothes well, and Charley just ruined them. This was incredibly not the time for processing that.

"Hmm. I've been doing some rituals to try to get information about her, and that's the strongest thing that comes through, but it could be I've misunderstood. Would she have been wearing something nice when she vanished?"

"I can't see why. She wasn't when she came home, anyway."

"Alright. Let me know what you find out about the fish. You can text me if you like."

Charley looked up, evidently with a surprised expression on her face.

"Oh, don't look so shocked I have a phone, child, I even have a laptop, though I don't use it too much. But you think having a website is going to do me good, or you think it's going to cause me a whole lot of trouble? Here's my number. Don't pass it on – if you do I'll drown you."

Charley thought she was joking. Thought. Wasn't going to find out though. She took the number.

Back in the cabin, after eating a very processed muffin that apparently didn't expire for two more years, Charley decided it was well past time for a trip for supplies. Even if she didn't go as far as Dunedin, she'd be able to get some basic clothes and do a supermarket trip in Balclutha. But first, she wanted to see if she could find anything online about the fish she'd seen; semi-translucent, brightly-coloured fins, a mass of them swimming around.

After a few minutes, Charley sighed in frustration. Maybe her search engine skills were lacking, but her attempts were proving about as useful as the fish poster. Of course, they might be purely imaginary fish, and no more significant than a messed-up stress dream.

She shut the laptop lid. She supposed it might be a good idea to go and see this Lawson after all.

She started to get up and then she looked down at herself, slightly confused, almost dazed. On what planet was knocking on someone's door – a stranger's door no less, and unannounced – even remotely preferable to searching for something online? And yet before she knew it she was shoving her feet back into her shoes, putting her sunglasses on, and heading for the holiday park office to get directions.

The sign was up to say Gordon was elsewhere on site, and rather than pushing the buzzer she went off to find him, wandering around the park. It must be full of life once the season got underway – there was a pool and playground equipment and bench sets near barbeques. Now, though, even the permanent residents were nowhere to be seen.

She found Gordon putting up some hooks in one of the other cabins.

"Hi, Gordon," she said. "Do you happen to know someone called Lawson?"

"Aye, lives just across the river. What do you need him for?"

"Thalassa suggested I go to see him. It's a long story, but essentially I want his help identifying a fish." Gordon turned. His grey-white beard was freshly trimmed and he was dressed in a polo shirt with the logo of the park on the left. He rubbed his face, a signet ring briefly glinting in the afternoon sunlight.

"Oh, for sure. That is rather up his alley, isn't it? Walk with me and I'll show you."

From the edge of the campground, the house was visible across the river; a single-storey weatherboard dwelling, like most of them, with a green door and window frames. Charley thanked Gordon, took a breath, and then headed over there, knocking on the door. A person perhaps Charley's age, perhaps a bit younger, answered it. Their skin was a mid-brown, their black hair cut into a careful bob. They wore black dungarees over a purple T-shirt.

"Hi, I'm looking for Lawson."

"We're all Lawsons, but you're probably after my dad. I'm Anahera. They/them."

They tapped the badge they were wearing with just those pronouns, then held out their hand which Charley accepted. "Charley. Uh, she/her, I guess. I'm not sure, I was told he could help me identify a fish."

"That's definitely Dad." They turned to call into the house. "DAD!"

A man approached, heavy-set and wearing green plaid flannel. "What's up?"

"This is Charley. She wants you to help identify a fish."

Lawson raised his eyebrows at Charley. "Let's see it, then."

"Uh. I don't have it, sorry. I'm not even sure it's local. Thalassa back there said if I told you about it you could identify it."

"I probably can. Let me guess, you magicked up a vision."

"Uh, so it was a dream. I don't know if it means anything, but... okay, so my sister is missing, and I've got to give anything a go."

"Fair enough, fair enough. I don't believe in all the woo woo but she is good at working stuff out, so you haven't made a bad decision there. Take a seat."

Charley perched on a bench on the porch, her back to the road, and Lawson took the old armchair. It had clearly been pink once, but little trace of those days remained, and the chair creaked when he sank his body into it.

"Tell me about this fish," he said.

Charley did her best, but it was hard to pull out features from a memory of a dream that was constantly moving. Still, it didn't take her long before he had grabbed a book from inside and was leafing through the pages.

"Like these?" he asked, holding out the open book. "They're translucent in a way that doesn't come across well in a picture."

Charley squinted at the page. It was hard to translate the vivid, slightly surreal motion of her dream to this still and solid water colour, but they were undoubtedly the same creature. "Yes, those!"

"It's the yellow and black on the fins that gives them away. They're Pristella Maxilaris, water goldfinches. Won't find them near here though, unless they're in a tank – coastal waters off South America is more like it."

Charley double-checked the spelling before texting Thalassa. Then, thanking Lawson, she walked back along the single-lane road, across the bridge, and then down to the beach. This time, though, she sat on the rocks looking out to sea. She took out her phone again – there was no response from Thalassa, but she didn't really expect one. She could figure this out though. She was good at puzzle games, and maybe this was the same skill. She searched for the Latin name she'd been given and pulled up the relevant Wikipedia page. It seemed this one fish had quite a few nicknames. And one, in particular, caught her eye: the x-ray fish.

She texted Thalassa: "The fish are x-ray fish. My sister did a placement in radiology. Coincidence???"

"Maybe not," came the reply.

It didn't feel much like coincidence at all.

Charley felt as if she was on the edge of something, but she wasn't sure in which direction she was going to end up falling. The answers hadn't come together yet, but she was making headway. And she wanted to talk about that, and not with Thalassa.

The house was towards the back of Inver Aora, just before the hill began to abruptly slope upwards. It was an ordinary weatherboard home, neither small nor large, one that would have benefited from a bit of paint, as would many, but not one that had yet reached a state of disrepair. There was a low plastic slide and a single swing on the front lawn, a smattering of toys amid the grass. A small cottage peaked out from behind, at the far end of the section.

Charley knocked on the door. True answered it, a toddler on her hip. Behind her stretched a narrow corridor with rooms off to each side, and a kitchen with large windows clearly visible at the far end. Another child scampered out from one side of the corridor and watched them, leaning against a doorframe.

"Hey, uh. Thank you for being kind to me yesterday. I was just letting everything get to me."

"Oh, no worries. Just glad you didn't end up in the river." She wiped the mouth of the toddler with a tissue. "You okay?"

"Yeah, I am. I was just wondering. Can I ask you some questions about Thalassa?"

True stepped inside to allow Charley to enter. "Go for it."

"When you said longer than any of us can remember," Charley said carefully, "just how long do you mean?"

"Go play in your room for a bit," True said to her older child, opening a door to her right and guiding them into a room with bunk beds and dangling strips of glittery fabric hanging from the ceiling. She adjusted the toddler in her sling, probably praying that it wouldn't require her attention. Then she opened another door and motioned Charley in. Charley looked around in wonder.

Books lined the room from ceiling to floor, corner to corner. The shelves were an odd mix – most of them seemed to be bracketed to the wall, some of those sagging in the middle, but there were also regular bookcases shoved against the walls, with bookends on top, and other shelves erected in between as if it had been gradually altered to accommodate someone's growing book collection until that collection took over the entire room.

In the middle were a couple of desks, again shoved together, and yet they looked expensive. One had a globe on, the countries and oceans of the world in tones of brown. It had to be there just for the aesthetic. Not that that bothered Charley as such, but it was a bit of a contrast with the books that had clearly been – and were there to be – read. They were paperbacks and books with broken spines, faded in patches, and they were of different heights and stacked up on each other. It wasn't that they weren't cared for – it seemed to Charley that they were – but they weren't just for display.

"I didn't think you'd have books like this," said Charley.

"You think some young parent dropout can't have a lot of books?" True asked.

Charley felt her face burning up. "I'm sorry, I didn't mean, I..." She hadn't meant that, but she said things she didn't mean so often she was past the point she felt she could be excused. Sometimes she felt like she was looking at them all, a dirty, messy, tangle of mistakes and hurt.

"I know you didn't. But be extra careful not to make assumptions around here. You won't get on well if you do."

It was one of several moments Charley had had since arriving where she wanted to ask for an explanation but had found things had moved on for everyone else. In this case, True was running her finger along a shelf of books.

"This was my grandfather's library," she said, "though he's been gone since I was little. I've been adding to it, these past few years, cataloguing things – he had a list of everything in here but nothing computerised. Some of it is just things he read and enjoyed. Like there's a whole stack of crime novels, I lend them out sometimes – the nearest actual public library is an hour away and we're not in zone for it so you have to pay, so some of the older people appreciate me doing that, and I grab things at book sales as well. But a lot of this is pretty rare – not valuable, but just really local things that nowhere else hangs onto, and... aha!"

True pulled a volume from the shelf and opened it on the table. "Okay, this is a book of poetry by a schoolteacher who grew up here, he wrote it soon after the first world war. And somewhere in here..." she flicked through the pages. "Ah, here."

She read it aloud:

"*The white-haired lady with the driftwood staff Against the tide contends; we dare not laugh.*

"That's part of a description of the town from 1921."

"And it sounds like she was already old at that point," Charley observed.

"It's possible it's not the same person. Maybe the same family have a habit of growing old and being mysterious up there, for whatever reason. It's the most rational explanation for it."

"Do you believe there's a rational explanation?" Charley asked.

True shrugged. "All I know is there's a fair bit we don't have an explanation for yet. That's all I can say."

The two of them were interrupted by the sound of running, and the pre-schooler burst into the room, yelling excitedly for his mother. True stepped forward and scooped him up, swinging him upside down as he laughed uproariously.

"I don't let them in unsupervised in case they pull the wrong thing out and it all crashes down."

"Wise," Charley observed.

"Anyway, yeah. If you have questions about the history round here, the answers are probably in this archive somewhere. If you want to know about the wildlife, especially marine life... have you met Lawson?"

Charley nodded. "Was sent to ask him a question about fish, actually. I met him, and his kid I think. Adult child."

True nodded in recognition. "Oh yes, that's Anahera – they? They'll just have finished their first year at uni. They started in February. Not even to Otago but all the way up to Auckland. Anyway, for the past two years the urge to get away has been actually radiating from them. I was honestly surprised they even came back to visit, let alone stay the whole summer. But I suppose some time away must have changed their perspective a bit."

Charley shrugged. "They seemed happy enough, as far as I could tell."

"A lot of people leave and never come back here. That's not news to anyone – few people can spend their lives in a place like this. But I think most of them find they miss it, at least at times. But also with all the excitement and busyness of their time in Auckland, Anahera will have had the chance to get a lot of stuff out of their system."

"Uh-huh." Charley could remember that age well. Her hometown had been much larger, officially a city even, but that sense of being ready for so much more, of being bursting to leave, was so familiar. Unlike those from here, she didn't miss it at all.

Charley was on her way back to her cabin when she realised she hadn't made it to Balclutha after all, that she was out of clean clothes, and her only source of food remained the limited options sold in the holiday park which were starting to make her feel a little twitchy. She swore under her breath. She had just been going to do it – how could she have forgotten entirely?

She supposed, as she grumpily threw her clothes in the washing machine and pushed coins into the slot, that this was the executive functioning issue she'd read about, except it felt like something more than that. She perched on the bench, barefoot and wearing as few clothes as decency would allow, and watched the clothes turning in the machine, over and over, tossed and turned within the water.

Chapter Five

In the morning, rather than Charley having to make her way up the long winding path to Thalassa's hilltop home, for once Thalassa came to find her. Charley was playing games on her phone, missing her consoles back home – a little selfish, she knew, to be missing video games at a time like this, but they were what distracted her, the one thing she was good at. She heard the knock on the door and pulled back the curtain to see Thalassa casting a dramatic presence, with her staff and her long hair and her billowing clothes, even in the more normal environment of the holiday park. Charley wondered how she'd be perceived in the city – a bit of a nutter, probably – but here, here this was her domain. And she had news for Charley.

"I've got someone who works for the hospital calling me back. Good lead on the radiology... ah, here they are."

Thalassa answered the phone and explained, in vague terms, that she was an investigator contracted by the family. Then she put the phone on speaker, placed it on an unoccupied bunk and turned up the volume.

"I have Melissa's sister Charley here with me."

"Hi, Charley." The woman sounded harried.

"Hi," Charley responded, her mouth dry.

"What can you tell us about Melissa and your interactions with her in the week before she disappeared?" Thalassa asked. There was a pause, and Charley wondered if they were actually going to get any useful information.

"There was something," she said hesitantly. "I didn't mention it at the time because it didn't seem relevant, and I was worried the cops might misinterpret it. But I'd been going over it in my mind, and when you contacted us again – well, if there's a possibility we might find her..."

"Go on," Thalassa said.

"A couple of days before she went missing a patient said he'd had some jewellery stolen. I had to speak to Melissa about it."

"She wouldn't steal," Charley interjected.

"I didn't think so either. It's quite possible the patient was confused, to be honest, but I had to talk to her. I wasn't accusing her, it was more just have you seen anything, but Melissa got really upset about it."

"Angry?" Thalassa asked.

"No, upset-upset. Almost kind of teary. But you have to understand, the long hours we expect of these students, it's not unusual for a small thing to be too much at some point."

"Did you find out what happened to the jewellery?"

"No. As I said, it's possible the patient wasn't wearing it that day or lost it some other place."

"Can you describe the jewellery to us?"

There was a long pause. "I'm sorry, I don't think I can. It was so distinctive I'd risk identifying the patient. I was more just concerned about... well, Melissa's state of mind. I hope she was just a bit tired and sensitive and nothing more... do let me know if you find her."

"Of course," said Charley.

"Well there's a lead," Thalassa said, after the call had finished.

"You think Melissa went missing because she was upset someone suggested she might have taken some jewellery?" Charley asked, sceptically.

"No. But I think this patient has some pertinent information for us. I'm going to make a call to a hospital contact."

Twenty minutes later, Thalassa had both a name and an address for the patient.

"So they won't describe the jewellery because it might identify the patient, but someone else will just identify the patient, got it. How much of what you do is magic versus having a whole network of people who owe you favours?"

"The real question is, how much of what I do is doing people favours using magic so they'll owe me in return? Anyway, they're in Balclutha, no need to go all the way up to Dunedin. We'll take my car, I'm not sure yours is roadworthy."

Charley was about to object – her warranty was up to date, and really, what sort of car did Thalassa expect her to have on a part-time retail wage? But Thalassa was already walking down towards her car. Charley followed her, getting in the passenger side. The car was relatively normal, a recent model but nothing showy. There were some bits of sea glass around, but nothing more than that. Thalassa reversed out, back on to the main road, and then they were moving.

The radio crackled in and out of reception. Charley couldn't even imagine what Thalassa's era of music would be – classical? Music hall? The station she had it tuned to was much more recent, though, a lot of the eighties' and nineties' music Charley's parents listened to. They left the sea behind them, heading for the larger settlement, a town perhaps but not a city, further up a larger river. They came to a halt in front of a house, the address they'd been given.

"Wow," Charley said. Amid the single-storey weatherboard homes, this one stood out. It was older, perhaps, and definitely larger. Surrounded by trees, it was two storeys, three if you counted the windows in the roof with – were those turrets at the corners? Everything from the edging around the windows to the chimney stack made it clear this was a fancy place. It wasn't at its best – the paint was peeling, and the trees at the front were a bit overgrown, but it still looked more than liveable. And Charley could imagine it taking a lot – both in energy and money – to maintain something like this.

Thalassa was out of the car and halfway up the path by the time Charley had undone her seatbelt. She scrambled after her.

The door was opened by an older man, who seemed to have shrunk inside clothes too big for him. Thalassa handed him a card.

"Mr Richard Ansley? My name's Tal, I'm a private investigator. I've been tasked with looking into a series of thefts from the hospital. This is Lottie, my assistant." Charley winced at the nickname she'd narrowly avoided as a kid. It would have been nice if they could have agreed on names in advance.

"Well, I'm glad someone's taking it seriously. Please come in."

The room they were shown into was old-fashioned but clean. The furniture was mostly dark wood, with burgundy fabric; there was a wall of leatherbound books, various artwork which included a series of photos – children and grandchildren, perhaps – and at least two taxidermied creatures. Large seashells sat on top of a dresser. Charley would have loved to explore this house, to find out its secrets.

"Some tea please, Laura," he said to the young woman hovering in the doorway. A granddaughter, or... could he really have a servant?

The three of them settled down on comfy seats, and Charley nibbled on some shortbread.

"Can you tell us when you last saw the ring?" Thalassa asked.

"I had to take it off for the x-ray. I put it with my things, on this shelf in the little room they told me to get changed in. When I got back it was gone." He seemed faintly outraged, as if he were the sort of person the used to having his own way.

"That's troubling. Do you have a picture of it?"

He took one out of a drawer. "Took this for the insurance. It's not replaceable really, though."

The first thing Charley thought was that she could understand why the guy was upset at having lost the ring, because it was beautiful. It was a signet ring with a large jewel that shone blue and turquoise, and even in the photo it seemed to ripple like the waves of a tropical sea. Over the stone was a tiny, but detailed, metal spider, eight spiny legs spreading out to the edges.

There was something about it she couldn't quite put her finger on.

Thalassa got his permission to take a photo with her phone, while asking him a little more about his visit to the hospital. Charley poured herself a cup of tea, while Laura hovered in the doorway. She zoned out a little wondering about the ring until Thalassa's voice grabbed her attention again.

"Where did you get the ring from?" Thalassa asked.

"Oh, you know, we've had it a long time. Now, thank you for coming, but I really must rest after my recent illness. Please let me know if you make any progress."

He stood and ushered them to the door, in a way that made it ab- solutely clear there would be no more questions. Charley and Thalassa walked quickly down the garden path.

"...so the circle was a ring, and the eight were the spider legs," Charley said as they got in the car.

"Very good. And he's hiding something about it. Now before we try to work out what that is, do you need anything while we're in town?"

"Yes please, I was going to ask to get some groceries. And maybe stop at the Warehouse as well, if there's time." Charley rubbed her eyes. "But there's something else. I think I've seen that ring before."

Thalassa raised an eyebrow at her. "You know, I think I have too. Can't think where, though."

Under the door of Charley's cabin was a dinner invitation from True. Charley felt her shoulders tense as she read it. She wasn't sure if it was a pity invite, because True genuinely wanted her company, or because she was curious and wanted to find something out. This was increasingly feeling like the sort of place everyone had secrets. Irrespective, there was no way she was going to pass up the opportunity. She refused to allow herself to consider whether her enthusiasm was because she wanted to spend time with True, or because even though she now had some real food, the idea of someone else cooking for her, in a proper kitchen, almost made her want to cry.

After stowing the unchilled food in her cabin, she put the milk, cheese, and sliced meat along with the salad greens in the dining hall's shared fridge, hoping the quiet of the holiday park would mean it stayed there. With this, she'd be having something closer to proper meals: sandwiches and toast and cereal, and she had pasta and a jar of sauce for the evenings, along with a pack of microwaveable curry and some roti. It felt a little weird – accepting she was here for a while – but she was so sick of the breakfast packs and noodles that it barely registered. Then she brushed her hair, put on one of the new T-shirts she'd bought in Balclutha, and a cardigan over the top that made it seem a bit nicer, and walked up to True's house.

"Gran's taken the kids," True said. "She lives just down there, in the cottage behind us. I've got some chicken, and I'm roasting some kumara in the oven, then I'll just do some vegetables and gravy. Sound good?"

It actually sounded amazing, and Charley expressed that with enthusiasm. The kitchen was compact, but it just fit a four-seater table, pushed against one wall and presumably pulled out as needed. Charley reckoned it was a three-bedroom house – if so it was a hell of a choice to dedicate a full room to books, especially with two children. Not what she'd have prioritised herself, but it seemed comforting.

Having offered to help and been declined twice, Charley leaned against the kitchen doorframe, chatting as True prepared the meal.

"So, 'True'? Is that one of those puritan virtue names?"

True's brown eyes glinted as she looked up.

"Ha! Well it's after my great grandmother – my mother was very close to her, and her name was Ermintrude, but my mother wasn't quite close enough to her to saddle a child with that, so she shortened it to True for me. I went through a stage of not liking it, but I've grown into it. The kids though – both their names are in the top 10 for their year of birth and I wouldn't have it any other way. Ollie and Allie, for now, they'll grow into Oliver and Amelia."

Charley smiled. "In a few years, they'll tell you they're sick of being one of three in the class and want to be acknowledged more as individuals. You can't win!"

"Not in the local school; it only has 30-odd students in a good year. They'll have all the individuality they want. But yes, I am resigned that no matter what choices I make at some point in their lives my kids will resent me for it. I think that's the only wholly predictable part of parenting."

"True's a good name, anyway."

"Thanks! You're a Charlotte, I assume."

"Yeah. My parents are... very like that. Guess my brother's name."

"Oh god, Sebastian?"

"Worse.

"Tarquin?"

"Okay, not that bad, he's a Rupert."

"Oh no. Like the bear?"

"Like the bear. He got a scarf for Christmas one year and he wasn't happy about it."

True served up the meal and took a seat. She listened to Charley talk about her sister, just tell her who she was in a way that wasn't about her height and hair colour which she'd had to repeat so many times it almost made her ill. They sympathised with each other about the families they'd grown up with, even though their parents seemed at near opposite ends of the spectrum. True told Charley about growing up here, mostly with her grandmother as her mother seemed incapable of staying in one place for more than a few months.

"Wasn't it a bit weird growing up with Thalassa here?" Charley asked. The meal was as good as she'd expected it to be, and well matched with the wine – the sort of thing Charley's parents cared about, but she hadn't quite expected to find in Inver Aora.

"Not really. I didn't know any different. Didn't you have any neighbourhood characters growing up?"

Charley thought. "I guess there was this hoarder guy. He used to abandon cars full of junk in different parts of the city, and his house was a maze of junk. Cats would go in there and reappear a week later having got lost amid all the stuff. It's kinda sad in retrospect, now I know that that stuff is usually a mental health thing, but he was just a strange guy to us."

"Yeah, like that. I mean, not the mental illness – she's got some weird beliefs, but I don't think she hallucinates, just like a lot of people have spiritual beliefs or whatever. Yes, she does things that seem impossible, but..." True shrugged. "It's hard to explain. I know the rest of the world takes a hard-line on what is and isn't possible and what magic is and isn't and how it doesn't really exist, but this is just our normal growing up here. I know it's difficult to understand."

It was difficult, Charley agreed with that, but she felt she was far closer to understanding than she would have ever thought possible. A couple of weeks ago she hadn't believed magic existed. Now she not only accepted it did, but was pretty unsurprised by each occurrence of it.

"So you got that doctor's appointment booked? For the ADHD stuff you were talking about?"

"Yeah," Charley said, looking down. "I just feel ashamed, like I had potential but I was too lazy to apply myself. I failed out of uni twice, for no good reason."

"It sounds like there may be a good reason."

"I know, but I'm scared of that too. That this has all been a waste, all been for nothing. Ugh, sorry, stuff going round in my head."

"It's all good. You're looking at the girl who had potential and ended up a teenage pregnant dropout. You can talk to me about this."

Charley rubbed her eyes. "I think I'm going to fail polytech now as well. Even before all this happened, I don't think I'd have passed."

"I mean, that sucks, but also the education system's a bit bullshit. The whole idea everything depends on decisions you make when you're still in your teens. I reckon you'll get there, even if it takes a while."

Charley nodded. It reminded her of the sort of faith her sister had in her, faith she didn't want to disappoint. "Do you often do the night-time walks?"

"Yeah. Clears my head. Gran keeps an eye on the kids and I get some headspace. Some days it's all I get – the days are chaos."

"I can imagine. I can't even care for myself properly. But I guess you were never this chaotic just by yourself."

"I was the nerd. I was how people think of Anahera now – I was going to get far out of here, I was going to be a success. And then I got pregnant when I was 16. Enrolled in correspondence school. Did okay, redeemed myself a little in some people's eyes. Got into university. Tried moving to Dunedin, leaving Ollie with Gran, coming back every second weekend. Loved the study. Everything else was unbearable. Got pregnant again, and if you think it's bad the way people look at you with one... Well with one, people think there but for the grace of God go I, but with two they think you've fallen into some deep pit and your life is a self-made tragedy forever."

"It's so bad people think like that. Kids are great."

"Thank you. I think so too. Kids *are* pretty great, and yes, my two could have come along at a more convenient time, but hey, life would be boring if it didn't take you by surprise now and then. And I'm still planning to get a degree, by correspondence, when Ollie's at school and Allie's a bit older so I can leave her when I go to block courses. But I think I'm staying here. I can't be the sort of someone I'd be elsewhere, but I can maybe be the someone I want to be. I reckon you can too."

Charley tried her best to sleep well. She'd opened the window of the cabin – she felt perfectly safe, and it was officially a shared cabin in any case – to let the night in and cool things down a bit.

There was a lot to think about. Whatever had happened to Melissa. Her weird fish dream that apparently wasn't just a normal dream. The idea there was a reason she struggled with so many things and it wasn't just being lazy. And then there was True.

True with that striking beauty, the straight-backed walk. It wouldn't surprise Charley at all if there wasn't a little bit of magic to it. Despite the utter normalcy – which she had appreciated – of their conversation today, True didn't seem to entirely come from this world.

True... True was weird in ways Charley couldn't quite put her finger on. Probably not supernaturally weird, though she supposed she couldn't rule anything out anymore, but something that was hard to specify and yet definitely there. She didn't seem to operate quite in the same world as Charley, didn't seem to work quite in the way she did, and yet Charley had to admit that she was intriguing.

Intriguing and possibly attractive?

Charley laughed. Oh good lord no. That was literally the last thing she needed right now. Soon, she expected, very soon, Inver Aora and all the people who inhabited it would seem like a hazy memory, a surreal dream, a weird blip outside the main narrative of her life. Soon things would be normal again, and she was looking forward to it more than she could say.

Mostly.

Chapter Six

"Morning," Gordon called out as he entered the combined kitchen and dining room, which was itself largely its own building. It was still empty except for Charley – the permanent residents did their own thing, she imagined, mostly living in campervans that had at least basic kitchen facilities. It felt empty, all these tables between her and the door, but she wasn't paying much attention to that as she dug into her cereal. Her milk had miraculously survived and she had her childhood comfort cereal, Froot Loops, straight from the supermarket, and after the past few days of cardboard-tasting breakfast packs from the holiday park reception, she felt renewed and like anything was possible.

"Hi," she replied, planting her spoon in her bowl. The box was next to it in the hope she'd manage to take it back to the cabin with her.

"Don't suppose this is yours?" Gordon asked, approaching and holding out his hand. In it, Charley could see a bracelet, a plain silver chain. She picked it up and held it up to the light. "I found it on the floor in reception."

"It's not mine," she said after a pause, "but it's like one my sister has."

"A sign from her, perhaps?" he suggested, so gently Charley had to force down hope.

"Maybe," she said, offering it back. "But it's a really common…"

And then, as their hands met, she saw it. The ring, the swirling blue colours, and the eight legs of the spider branching out. The blue seemed dulled and faded, more so than that of the missing one she'd only seen in a photograph, and yet they were unmistakably the same design. She felt her heart start to beat really fast, told herself to stay calm.

"Uh, if it's okay I'll take the bracelet and ask some of Melissa's friends if they can verify."

"Of course. It could have been around a while and I doubt it's valuable. Just bring it back if it turns out not to be and I'll put it in the lost property drawer."

As soon as he had gone Charley pulled out her chair and stood up in a rage. Gordon was part of this. Either he was involved in her sister's disappearance, or he knew who had been. Fuck. Up until this point she'd clocked him as someone kind, and now it turned out it was all a fraud.

She looked at the cereal in front of her, and took a deep breath. *Okay, Charley, you can do this. Make a sequence.*

Eating came first. She basically gulped it down and drank the remaining milk from the bowl. If this was a time for returning to childhood favourites then she could indulge in childhood habits too. Then she rinsed the bowl and spoon, picked them up along with the cereal packet, and returned to her cabin, flinging them and herself on the bed. Nervous, anxious energy was still coursing through her, but sequencing the past few actions had somehow taken the ability to do anything with it.

She was so sick of being so useless.

She lost track of the next two hours, but eventually she made it up the hill to Thalassa's place, and half-collapsed on one of the dining room chairs, relating what she'd learned.

"That man," Thalassa said. "Old enough to retire and still keeping childish secrets from me. You'd think he'd know better."

Charley let herself feel like she was sinking into her chair. "Do you think he can help us?" she asked, feeling herself calm a little as she said it. "He couldn't have... I mean, he wouldn't have done something to her, would he?"

"Kidnapped her? It's always good to be suspicious, but I can't imagine it. I think it's more likely that one is oblivious to just what he's connected to than that he's some sort of mastermind."

"Masterminds don't do their own dirty work, though," Charley said.

"And that's true. I can only tell you what my gut's saying at this point. And if there's a way to use him to find your sister I'm going to find it, don't you worry about that."

Thalassa's attention turned to the bracelet. She looked at it with one eye closed, and then through a magnifying glass.

"Are you sure this is your sister's?" she asked Charley. She pushed a bowl of tamari almonds in her direction. "Eat those, you'll be hungry."

"I don't know how I can be sure. But it looks just like it, and it would be one hell of a coincidence." Charley stuffed some almonds into her mouth. She had no idea how Thalassa could tell things like when she was hungry better than she could – witchcraft at once didn't seem reason enough and seemed complete overkill for such a question.

"Well I can see some trace of salt crystals on it. Hmm. I think you need to do some meditation. Have you done that before?"

"I've tried. My mind keeps wandering."

"And then you stress yourself out trying to stop it?" Thalassa guessed. She got up and Charley followed her through the house to a room she hadn't seen before. It was dimly lit and near empty – the only furniture a low chair and a table with drawers beneath. Out of one drawer Thalassa withdrew a large candle and lit it, then placed it on the table.

"I'll be gone a while," she said. "You just focus on the bracelet. Don't try to logic anything out, there's nothing to logic – it's just a simple bracelet. Work from instinct, empty your mind, let what you can intuit flow into your brain. Don't rush it."

The candle flickered in front of Charley, the bracelet glinting on the table between them. Shadows seemed to try to form around the room and then fell into nothingness. She tried to keep her focus on the nothing at the centre of the candle flame, but everything kept tugging at different parts of her brain. Where *was* Melissa and how had this bracelet ended up coming back to her? What was Thalassa up to? What was *True* doing right now? Oh god, had someone at work discovered her little book of worst customers that her friends used to read for laughs? Did anyone actually figure out what was wrong with the Slushie machine? How long was it until her last assignment was due and was there even the slightest hope of making it through the year?

Bracelet. Focus. She could do this.

Was this really Melissa's bracelet, and if so, how did it get here? What was happening when she lost it – oh god, did someone take it from her? How does one distinguish different bracelets from each other? Do they have serial numbers? You could probably tell by DNA left on it; should she have brought Melissa's hairbrush with her?

But finally, things began to change. Instead of giving up, instead of panicking, she found herself able to drift into story. She found herself on open seas, land only visible in the distance. Birds circled overhead – seagulls, perhaps even an albatross, and even this far out a few ducks were sitting on the water. Charley breathed in and out, trying to focus, trying to look beyond what she saw.

There was something shadowy moving just out of the corner of her eye. An impression of long, spindly legs, like a giant insect creeping towards her. Charley felt her heart rate going up, fear clutching her. She was starting to panic, breathing fast, wanting to be out of this place as much as she wanted any information to be revealed.

The candle went out. The room plunged into darkness.

Not knowing if she'd succeeded or failed spectacularly at the task she'd been assigned, only that her heart was beating extremely fast, Charley made it down the path of the cottage, heading for the closest thing to a safe place she had here: her holiday park cabin. The vision played in her mind, dreamlike and disconcerting. It felt more real than something only imagined, and even here, in broad daylight, she didn't feel entirely safe. How could she protect herself from something she didn't understand?

For now, though, she just made her way through the little settlement that had become familiar to her, with its river and cluster of houses. Low cloud had descended on the holiday park, so dense Charley could barely see the entrance, while the air around was clear. She paused, taking in what she knew must not be a natural phenomenon, before making her way down the driveway.

Every sound had her on edge. She turned, side to side, in the thick fog, seeing – or thinking she could see – things out of the corners of her eyes. Uneasy dreams played just outside her vision, insectoid legs stretching and stalking around her. She breathed deeply and pushed on, the cloud thinning to a clear stretch of land in the centre of the holiday park.

Just ahead of her, Thalassa and Gordon faced each other, sidestepping, angling for a fight. Wisps of cloud swirled around their feet and then dissipated into the thick fog that encircled this arena. They both looked furious.

"You asshole. There is no good reason for you to be hiding this from me. Tell me what the ring means!"

"It's just an old thing, okay? It's none of your business."

A handful of spectators had gathered around the far side of the clearing. Charley noticed True amongst them, her arms folded and expression wary. A couple more of the park's permanent residents emerged from their caravans, edging forward and peering through the fog, as if they'd never seen something so exciting, nor had so much fun, in all their lives.

"Do not lie to me!" Thalassa bellowed. She was tiny, she was elderly, but she was a force to be reckoned with. She stalked forward, slamming her staff into the ground with every step. Gordon edged backwards, sliding himself behind the climbing frame. Charley couldn't tell if he was reluctant to fight a woman because it felt unchivalrous, or if he was genuinely scared of what she might be capable of.

"Thal…" Charley tried to say, but she got nowhere. Thalassa was already on a rant and it seemed like there was no stopping her.

"You're useless. You're rude. You have no respect for your elders."

"Oh, useless am I? Well, there's a new one. I host your guests, even find room for them in the height of summer. I help you fix your car. Just once I require a little privacy, I don't give you everything you want, you…"

Shimmering light emerged from Thalassa's hand, coalescing into a ball which she threw at Gordon, a gleaming trail lingering in its wake. With a look of horror, or perhaps fury, he dodged what was coming for him. It sputtered into sparks and then died away, leaving smoke filling the air.

Gordon picked himself up. "Go back to your witch castle, you silly old bat!"

Charlie crouched behind a slide as another bolt of blue whooshed through the air. Gordon dodged, stumbling against a picnic table that thumped onto its side. Charley suspected he'd once been agile, perhaps an athlete. And it wasn't so much that he was limited now, even though he appeared to be pushing retirement age – his job was, after all, pretty hands-on – so much as he hadn't adjusted and still on some level expected himself to be as spry as he'd been when he was young. The effect could have been comedic, but Charley found herself wincing. She wasn't yet sure what to make of Gordon – his earlier kindness and the possibility he might in some way be keeping them from finding Melissa jostled for space in her head – but she took no pleasure in seeing him like this.

He certainly wasn't helpless though. Pulling himself up, he picked up a large spiral screw – the sort used for securing trampolines – and threw it at Thalassa, who stepped neatly out of the way.

Charley watched anxiously, unsure what she wanted the outcome to be, except to hope it didn't delay her search. She suspected *this* was as much about their respective personalities and, more to the point, their longstanding friendship with each other as it was about Melissa or about Gordon's ring or whatever Gordon was hiding from Charley and Thalassa both.

Frustration hung in the air, built up to explosion point. Thalassa threw two trails of turquoise which divided and ran round opposite sides of the climbing frame, forcing Gordon to drop to the ground.

"I haven't finished with you, Gordon Drever," she bellowed. Then quieter, "Come on, Charley, we've got work to do."

Charley mouthed an apology to Gordon, walking quickly to catch up with Thalassa as she strode into the fog.

"Shit," Charley said, still shaken, not together enough to feel like she shouldn't swear because it was like swearing in front of your grandmother. "You could have killed him."

Thalassa snorted.

"Pfft, what I was throwing was mostly light, minimal heat or other types of energy. Very little risk unless I'd got him in the eye at an odd angle or something."

Charley raised an eyebrow. The chances of that did not seem as negligible to Charley as Thalassa wanted them to sound, but there wasn't going to be any value in saying that. Even though Gordon seemed unharmed, and at worst the playground equipment would need some repairs, she didn't feel entirely comfortable knowing that forces like that existed in the world. Then again, given that they did, it was maybe good that she knew about it and that she'd established a relationship with a practitioner of them. In the absence of any clear answers, she followed Thalassa up to her house. The fog burned off as they walked, revealing a clear, blue-skied spring day.

"Seriously," Thalassa continued, as they approached the top of the path. "It's basic beginner's magic, far more show than substance. I reckon even you could learn to do it."

Charley didn't bristle at the remark, though she suspected it was designed to make her bristle. Instead, she just smiled and shook her head.

"I'm being serious. Okay. Try this. Sit down there."

Charley sat once more on the bench she had first sat on what seemed like an age ago, waiting for Thalassa to arrive, with no knowledge of what would happen next.

"Okay, you're going to use your mind to bring out a blue glow on your palm."

"Don't I need a spell or a potion or something?" Charley asked, disbelieving but nervous anyway.

"For more complex spells, sure. If you could ever go that far. But this one's simple. Okay, focus on the palm of your hand and try to draw energy from your body to it. Don't wonder how it works, just try to work a muscle you didn't know was there, channel the energy into your hand, that's it."

Charley tried to focus, felt like something moving inside her was growing, and then she lost it. She opened her eyes and shook her head.

"You're overthinking it. Stand up. Now take a step forward."

Charley was puzzled, but did so anyway.

"Right, so when you walked forward you didn't think 'I'll contract that muscle to raise my leg and then shift the balance of my body forward before straightening my knee and so on…' you don't think that crap. You just do it. So make a blue orb glow on your right hand."

Charley sat back down, took a deep breath and shut her eyes. She felt something shift, something tingle, as if muscles she'd never used before were waking and stretching, as if something new was flowing in her veins. She felt her skin crawling with sweat. Almost not daring to breathe, she opened her eyes. Resting on her palm was a glowing blue sphere. She hardly dared to blink. The more she looked at it the more complex it became, more hues than she could imagine swirling almost hypnotically in it. It was the most beautiful thing she had ever seen.

"See," Thalassa said. "Magic isn't an either-or thing. Most people have a bit of it in them if they try hard enough. You did well." She waved a hand and the orb disappeared into nothing.

Had it really ever been there at all? Had Charley really created it? It seemed so hard to believe, that everyone walking around could just do this if they simply set their minds to it, but Charley had seen it with her own eyes. All this potential magic ability out there, so little of it known or acknowledged or even imagined.

"Come along child, come in, stop dawdling."

Charley looked at the door. The scene inside – the wooden table and chairs, the tea cups, the art work – was remarkably unthreatening, and yet she was struggling.

"What is it, child?"

"It's... it's stupid but the thing I saw, when I did the meditating."

"What precisely did you see?"

"I don't know... it just scared me. There were... shadows. Legs. Not human legs. I was out at sea, with all these birds, and there were long legs, like an insect..."

"Interesting. But trust me, my spare room's not dangerous to you. Come in."

Charley was still shaking as she picked up her bag and walked inside, but Thalassa was following another train of thought.

"You know why he's like that?" Thalassa asked.

"Who?"

"Gordon. He threw a... what was that he threw at me?"

"Maybe a trampoline screw?"

"Right. I can't believe he'd do that, but you know why he's so obnoxious? Boarding school. People who went off to boarding school are honestly the most difficult to deal with, I swear. People who think the whole world revolves around some childish alliance or pinky promise they made when they were 15."

Charley asked, with what she hoped came across as genuine confusion, how that related to the ring, why it made Gordon difficult, if it could be any help in finding Melissa. Rather than responding directly, Thalassa brought her tea.

"There. That will help get your strength up. Magic in a beginner is exhausting. Make sure you eat and sleep well tonight."

This batch of tea – regular tea, not the apparently magical concoction – tasted good. It was sweet and minty and Charley sipped it gratefully, only half-listening to Thalassa's furious ramble about Gordon.

"So, my guess is he has loyalty to some cult or club or fraternity or whatever and thinks he secretly rules things. Does he really think they wouldn't drop him in it without a second thought if it happened to be expedient? He's a fool if you ask me."

"Uh huh," Charley said. "Do you mind if I pour myself some more tea?"

Thalassa sighed, and pushed the pot, on its little plaited fabric coaster, across the table towards Charley. It was still warm and felt like it warmed Charley up from the inside when she sipped it.

"It was the same ring though," Thalassa said. "I saw it. Just worn. I can't believe I didn't notice... hmmm."

"What?" Charley asked.

"Well, some things have... you maybe have heard it referred to as a glamour. It doesn't make them invisible as such, but it means you don't really notice them. That would explain why in all the years of knowing Gordon I've never noticed he wore such a distinctive ring. Yes, it's worn and could do with a polish, but that in itself doesn't explain it. Except... you noticed it."

"I mean, it didn't mean anything to me. I just remembered it when I saw the picture."

"Hmm. Okay, we're going to have to work this out. Take this to him, will you?" She handed Charley a small jar. "Tell Gordon I'm sorry if I actually caused him any distress. If I harmed his ego tied up in rituals of class supremacy and..."

Charley supposed this was Thalassa's idea of reconciliation.

"He'd probably appreciate the apology more coming from you," Charley suggested gently.

"Exactly. That's why I'm not going to give him the satisfaction..."

Thalassa's grouching was curtailed by a sharp knock on the glass of the door.

"Please," the newcomer said, as Thalassa opened it. "Can you help me find my son?"

Charley read him as an East Asian man, maybe in his fifties, obviously agitated. Probably not in the right frame of mind for pausing to read the sign. She lingered just long enough to see if there were any similarities between the cases. It seemed like there were not. Melissa was a fifth-year medical student, and Joe – the other missing person – an engineering apprentice in Wanaka. They were a vaguely similar age – and of course links couldn't be ruled out – but there was no sign of a pattern. No, this seemed like just some other poor soul who'd been directed to Thalassa in a moment of crisis. Charley sighed and set off down the hill to face Gordon.

Chapter Seven

The journey between Thalassa's house and the holiday park had come to feel almost like a routine commute over the past few days, even though she hadn't even heard of those places until recently. It would be strange when she left here, strange to think that one day soon she'd leave and probably never come back, never make that walk again.

Charley headed around to her cabin first, plugging her phone in to charge, before starting to look for Gordon. In the grounds, the outdoor furniture had been returned to an upright position. Anahera, dressed in mustard-coloured overalls, with a they/them pin and another depicting what Charley thought was probably a manatee, was sweeping up the pathway with a broom.

"Oh, hi!" Charley said.

"Hey. Sounds like a bit of shit went down."

"You could say that. Looks like everyone survived, though?"

"Yup, but Gordon's pissed off. Thalassa too, I reckon."

"Yeah."

"I'm working here over summer, just casually, getting some money saved. Wasn't supposed to be starting 'til December, but it's a few extra dollars. And it's not like there's anything better to do in… this place…" They looked round with faint disgust. "I think he could clean up himself, he's more just angry about the idea of doing so. He's in there if you need him." They gestured at the reception room.

Charley swallowed before opening the door to reception. It was hard to work out how to approach him, not knowing how connected he was to Melissa's disappearance, but she wasn't going to get anywhere if she avoided him. He was sitting behind the counter, looking a little annoyed with the world but otherwise none the worse for wear.

"This is from Thalassa," Charley said, holding out the jar of marmalade with a handwritten logo and a small piece of ribbon around the neck.

"Hmm, not poisoned is it?" he asked, looking it over.

"She seemed genuinely sorry," Charley said. "Just stubborn."

"Yeah, I think if she wanted to kill me she'd do it to my face. Watch me squeal. In that case please pass this onto her, but not my thanks." He reached into the cupboard at the back of the counter and pulled out a large carry bag. "Some more frames for her beehives. I picked them up from a friend on my trip over yesterday. I know some of hers are getting a bit old. Tell her it's not for her benefit, just for mine. I'm sick of being stung by the old wasp she is, don't want to be stung by her bees as well."

Charley shook her head. "You really are as bad as each other," she muttered.

"Yes," said Gordon. "But I'm more than a hundred years younger. Under the circumstances, I think I might be forgiven for a little immaturity, don't you think?"

Charley laughed, but without enthusiasm. Her instinct was to like Gordon. He seemed like a good guy, and he'd been kind to her. But he also might have been responsible for Melissa's disappearance, or at least withholding information that could help find her. And that was practically the only thing that was, in her eyes, completely unforgivable.

"Do you even know what that was all about?" he asked. "Other than her objecting to the school I went to when I was all of 13 years old."

Charley looked at him, surprised. Could he really not know? "It's my sister. We think she found one of those rings and it's connected to how she went missing?"

It looked like the blood drained out of him. "Oh god, I didn't realise it was that serious. I... Okay, I just need to talk to some people and check some things. But I'll help you, I promise."

Charley nodded and left without saying anything. She wasn't sure she trusted herself with speaking, wasn't sure how to react.

Oddly, she found herself walking down to the sea. There was the bush path leading inwards by the river and other tracks up into the hills, and of course she still had her car, she could go anywhere; but while just days ago she would have made every effort to avoid the sea, now she headed there naturally as if it was the only logical thing to do.

The sea was calm today, and the weather felt like it was on the edge of summer. Nothing remained of the earlier fog. Waves rolled in and then collapsed into white foam before they reached the sand. A light breeze blew inwards, rippling in Charley's hair. She was overdue for a haircut, but even at the best of times she'd keep forgetting or putting it off, and this was far from the best of times.

She walked a little along the edge of the tarmac, where it gave way to ancient rock, the bag of frames dangling from the crook of her elbow. She was struggling less every day being by the sea. The salt and the pervasive scent of seaweed in the air were becoming less distressing. It wasn't just a case of getting used to it, something was changing in her. She hadn't been far from the sea growing up in Tauranga – she'd spent longer than this right by the sea on one or other ill-fated family holiday when she'd ended up storming off angrily while her parents complained that Charley always ruined everything. This was something different that was happening.

It was almost like being by the sea didn't bother her at all.

To think she'd been so obsessed with avoiding it she almost went to study at Waikato, in one of New Zealand's few inland cities, pulled to Dunedin only by her sister's support. Dunedin wasn't bad – the city centre wasn't on the coast like Tauranga or Wellington or Auckland or... Jesus, why were so many cities built on the coast? And she had no reason to ever go down to the port, so it didn't really bother her, but it was significant enough to have made it not her first choice of city.

The tea Thalassa was sporadically providing definitely helped, but there was more going on than that. It was time for her to start asking some questions.

Thalassa was kneeling on a thin cushion, secateurs in hand, thinning out some of the plants that grew in the bed between the main house and the other two buildings – the shed and the little stand-alone unit she called the studio. She looked round when she heard Charley arrive, telling her to head in while she finished off the patch of garden.

This time Charley made the tea, and it was only tea. Supermarket tea bags, nothing magical. She looked at Thalassa as she waited for the jug to boil. This was who Charley had paid seven years of her life to. Seven years, without even checking her credentials.

"Any leads on the missing guy?" Charley asked, putting the bee frames on the table.

"Nothing concrete. I don't think there's anything unusual about his disappearance, but I did some divinations for him and gave him suggestions on where to look. Not much else I can do." Thalassa examined the frames. "I see someone thinks he can apologise in wooden squares. Well I've had worse in my life."

It was the segue Charley needed, even if it was a bit of a reach. She asked Thalassa the question she'd really been dwelling on. "So what is your story? How did you end up here, and how can you do magic and stuff like that?"

There was a long, seemingly endless pause.

"You don't have to tell me if it's private or something," Charley said, forcing herself not to tremble as she passed the cup and saucer across.

"You don't get much private round here, in a place like this. No such luck. Everyone knows everyone else's business. They'd do better in life if they would mind their own. But I can't curse them all. I will tell you the story if you'd like, though?"

"Yes please," Charley replied, sitting down and wondering if she had just gone and lumped herself in with those whose lives would be much better if they were to mind their own business. She wasn't sure it mattered. She was used to being judged and a little more wouldn't hurt her.

"A long time ago I washed up on this here shore. It will have been 1836 if I've done my calculations right. Before the treaty. The motu looked very different then, and changed very quickly. Of course, I was too young to understand any of what was, let alone to predict what was to follow. Less than a year old, too young to speak or remember even my name, tied to part of what had been a ship with strips of cloth as if in a desperate hope I'd survive. No information on where I came from. I've researched ships that were wrecked or believed wrecked around that time and found nothing. People used to guess at where I might be from: Spain, Italy, even Turkey. I suppose we'll never know. It doesn't matter anymore anyway – even if someone else survived the wreck, they'd be long dead."

"Right here, on this beach?"

"Right here, so I'm told. It's the closest I have to a home, I suppose. The sea is the closest I have to a parent. But someone must have tied me to that flotsam believing there was a chance I would live, and as it happened so I did.

"It was, I was told, pure chance that anyone found me, someone up here to fish, and this squalling half-dead baby on the beach, so cold I should have been dead and probably half-starved as well. They took me home and fed me up, and I was passed from home to home for a while, homes I don't remember but I assume treated me well. Later there was something more formal set up in Dunedin – not a children's home yet, but they paid people to foster us orphans. I got a couple of years schooling, on a ship would you believe, before they built an actual classroom.

"Anyway, I was sent from the last foster family to help a farmer's wife with many kids when I was 14, that's what they were training us up for. That was hard work, but they were good people, always plenty of laughs and plenty of kai on the table. One of her boys, a bit younger than myself – he fancied himself a bit of a scholar, was one of the first to go to the university when it opened. He had an idea what was going on with me, nicknamed me Thalassa after the Greek goddess, and it stuck. But I was always drawn back here, and as soon as I could, I returned."

"Did you ever marry?" Charley asked gently. It struck her she'd become much more confident talking to Thalassa, and Thalassa had become a lot more forthcoming in answering her questions.

"Me? No, no. There were men, of course. There probably would have been women had the times been different. I always said I'd think about marriage when I understood who I was better, and, well, here I am. Plus it's hard to make a lifelong commitment once you realise you're going to have such different lifespans. But anyway, that's enough about me. What about you, where are you from?"

"Oh, er, Tauranga, I guess. I was born there. Moved to Dunedin about two and a half years ago." It was a quick subject change, and she noted that Thalassa had said nothing about how she came to have magic. But still, she'd just revealed so much more than Charley had previously known.

"Before that. What's your heritage? Your genealogy? Your whaka-papa?"

Charley scratched the ground with her shoe.

"I don't know. Probably English. I think my granddad said part of our family was Scottish. All my grandparents were born here though, at least, Tauranga or Waikato, I think."

"Hmm. Look into that. You might find something interesting there. And even if you don't, it's good to know where things started. Where you're connected to. Magic is all about pulling the strings of existence, and some of the most powerful can stretch back a very long time. Also it's just good form to be able to say where you came from, understand?"

Charley could see Thalassa's indignation, but she sensed sadness behind it too. "I understand. I'll ask some of my family what they know when all this is over."

Thalassa nodded in Charley's direction, which Charley understood to mean something vaguely approximating a thank-you. You wouldn't get more than that out of Thalassa, she reckoned, and there wasn't really any use in trying.

"We are going to find your sister, you know. Gordon needs some time to calm down and get over nonsense from years ago. He's just being defensive. Not a bad one – I've known him since he was a pēpi, even if he spent a lot of his life elsewhere. This place draws nearly everyone back eventually, and he was no exception. Once he's had a stiff drink, a good night's sleep, and a filling breakfast, he'll be over here with information. Whatever he knows – and I don't think he's the enemy here, but I think he knows something – we'll find out soon enough."

"He told me he needed to sort some stuff out."

"Yes, well. He'll do what he needs to do to save face, but he'll come through eventually."

Charley understood not to push Gordon any more, but she was dammed if she was just going to kill time. Not that there was exactly much to do to kill time in this place, either. But she did know exactly where was a good place to go if she was looking for information.

True looked unsurprised to see her, while Ollie waved shyly from the middle of a loop of toy train track.

"So, what is it you want to know?"

"I was wondering if you could help me work out which boarding school Gordon went to. Gordon who runs the caravan park. I know it's random, but it seems like it might be important."

True scrunched up her face.

"It was one in Dunedin, wasn't it? Why not just ask him?"

"You saw his little fight with Thalassa, didn't you?"

"Good point!" True replied, pulling a fussing Allie onto her knee. "Mind you, they've been ticking each other off for a while, I don't think it really surprised anyone that they finally came to blows."

"Yeah, so he's not exactly being cooperative, given the circumstances, but it's important. Any ideas on how I can find out? Anyone who might know?"

Charley expected to be sent up some winding path to visit someone with a gruff voice who had known Gordon all his life but didn't really appreciate visitors. That seemed to be the norm in places like this. Instead True had another – better – idea altogether.

"Newspapers," True said, reaching over her daughter to log in to her laptop. "There's a good chance he ended up – maybe there was a rugby team or maybe he got a scholarship? Some of the local papers used to publish everyone who passed their exams, which was a bit stink for those who didn't I suppose, but they also used to publish all the divorces, which was worse. So there's a database called Papers Past; it's run by the National Library and they have searchable scans of all sorts. We can start by just plugging his name in and selecting a date range and seeing what comes up. How old do you reckon Gordon is?"

"Uhhh."

"Okay, well we don't need to be too precise, I'm going to say about 60 but we can plug in a whole range of dates. And we think it was Dunedin so I'll reduce it to Otago publications for now, but we might want to end up looking a bit wider. Okay, and here were go."

They both watched as the little wheel span round indicating that results were being generated. Then it moved to a display page where both of them ran their eyes up and down looking for results that might be relevant.

"Could that be him?" Charley asked, pointing as True scrolled through the results. "It says one of them is called Drever, though it doesn't give a first name."

"One of a group of sixth form students who fundraised for repair and restoration of the war memorial. Well, that gives us a year and three possible schools, and... let me check..." She searched fast. "Only two are boarding schools. Let's see if knowing that can help us narrow the search results down. There are a few here with sports teams, but look at this. It doesn't mention Gordon specifically – it doesn't mention anyone by name, but it's one of those schools."

It was an article with a headline that read: 'Scandal at School – Police Tight Lipped'. The actual text was very vague, several young people were caught indulging in "behaviour that doesn't fit the morals of this nation".

"Is that a euphemism?" Charley asked.

"No, I don't think so. There's some discussion of financial gain further down. I don't think it just means they were fucking or anything that innocuous. I think they were involved in an actual crime – I mean, what we would consider an actual crime – but the newspaper doesn't want to state what, or they've been told not to for whatever reason. I think if they were trying to find out it would be more rah-rah our reporters are on the case. Four boys."

"Well that doesn't feel coincidental."

"No, and let me try something else." True typed quickly. "Yeah, see, look, here's the exam results for that year and no sign of his name for either school. He either failed everything – which is unlikely at a school like that, if you're prone to failure they get rid of you long before that – or he was no longer there by that point."

"Doesn't necessarily mean he was one of those kids."

"No, for sure, and we're not even certain it's the same school. And it could be something like that happening – whatever that was – made his parents think badly of the school and move him somewhere else, for example. But it looks like we have something mysterious happening with members of Gordon's year group."

"Indeed," Charley said assuredly. "I don't suppose there's more we can find out about what the incident is?"

"You want me to follow that up, or did you just need the name of the school?"

Charley nodded, thinking. "I'm kind of interested in anything related. There's something going on and I don't know how it all connects up."

"Leave it with me and I'll see what I can find out tomorrow morning." True paused. "Look, do you feel safe? Like, I'm sure Gordon's fine and it was probably just someone had weed or something else where a giant mountain ended up being made of a molehill, but I know you're kind of alone here and you've been staying at his campground... let me know if you need somewhere to stay or if anything feels wrong, okay?"

Charley felt herself start to flush. It was kind but she felt terribly awkward. Somehow she managed to get her words out sounding fairly normal.

"Yeah. I think he's okay but will do. Thank you."

\#

Charley struggled to sleep that night. Every noise seemed loud in the quiet of the near-empty holiday park. She was uncomfortable on her thin mattress but didn't bother to move. She felt so far from home – if, indeed, Dunedin was home. Everything was starting to feel like a dream.

She held out her hand and tried to make the blue orb grow on her palm with no success. It occurred to her that maybe it was all a cheap trick. Probably magic didn't really exist, it was just an illusion with a combination of cheap special effects and suggestibility. But Melissa was still gone, and quite possibly in a dangerous situation – maybe at sea, maybe held captive – and what was Charley's alternative? To go back to social media postings and handing out fliers in the Octagon while knowing that she'd failed to follow the one actual lead she had? That didn't sound like any way to live.

Besides, if Thalassa didn't actually have powers then she couldn't actually take years of her life. Surely if she was a scam artist she'd extract all the money she could.

It was all such a mess that she didn't know what to think. Finally – finally – they had been getting somewhere, and having to put the brakes on now, to wait, to sleep, was unbearable. She wanted to rush out and find her sister, she wanted to force people to tell her what she knew.

But she knew waiting was her best chance. It just felt impossible.

Chapter Eight

Charley was woken by knocking on the door of the cabin. She groaned, looked at the leggings and T-shirt she'd slept in and decided they were sufficiently close to actual clothes to greet whoever it was in. She made it barefoot across the room and opened the door to daylight and Gordon, who was actually looking kind of sheepish.

"You ready to go? I think we need to go talk to Thalassa."

Even with the changes of underwear and socks and the couple of additional T-shirts she'd picked up from the Warehouse during her trip with Thalassa a couple of days before, Charley's choice of clothes was limited. In some ways, it was easier to manage them that way. Somehow, shaking, knowing she was on the verge of some relevant information, knowing that today might be the day she found her sister or lost her forever, she pulled on her jeans – that she probably needed to wash again, but they'd do for today – and grabbed her phone and the cabin key.

She didn't say anything to Gordon as she joined him outside and slipped on her shoes, or as the two of them walked up to Thalassa's place. She wasn't angry so much as she had no idea what to say. When Thalassa opened the door Charley expected her to throw something at Gordon, but instead she just raised her eyebrows and took a seat.

"Decided to show yourself, then."

"Don't push it, Thalassa," he replied, also sitting. Charley took the chair between them.

Gordon scratched his beard. "Right, so. I've been noticing a few things that are a bit weird, and now I think they might be related to what happened to your sister. I don't have the answer for you, but maybe you'll be able to use what I tell you." He took off his ring and presented it to them. It was so much clearer now, almost glowing blue and turquoise, glinting in the light. Just like the other one. "The Chelicerata Society. It was an old group, my recruiters said. Mostly members of established, well-to-do families, but one of my classmate's brothers was involved and he recruited a couple of us."

"That's a fancy name," Thalassa remarked.

Gordon shook his head. "We thought it was just a name for the group. To make it sound... intimidating."

"Listen to him. Same type of people who are in parliament talking about banning the gangs, and they've got their own patches..."

"Thalassa, please," Charley said, hoping her tone came across as more pleading than annoyed. She turned to Gordon. "What did you do?"

"Well, we had oaths and ceremonies and stuff. The usual secret society things."

Thalassa snorted. "Charley went to normal day school, and I barely went to school at all, you'll forgive us if we don't know what's normal in a secret society."

Charley's school had not, in fact, been normal, and only a combination of Melissa being a star student, even at 13, and her parents' money had gotten her admitted. For all the good that had done anyone. But she decided that this wasn't the time to be bringing that up.

"The society was involved in some dodgy stuff. It may have been the more dramatic kind of smuggling once, but by our time It was a very boring tax and duty evasion scam. I was a scholarship kid, but I got caught up with the entitlement of the others. Honestly, I think it was more about getting one over on the government than making money for them, but it was about belonging, and yes, about the money for me. The rest of my family needed it.

"But the older ones, they talked about worshipping the spider like it wasn't a joke. They weren't taking the piss, y'know, and it wasn't just a symbol. They told stories about how it was a serious smuggling ring back in the day, and they used magic to transport goods somehow. Of course, we felt they were just getting on a bit, either that or messing with us. We mostly just wanted something exclusive to be part of.

"But then we got careless, and some of us got caught. The older members of the society helped out with legal stuff and we did a deal, so I didn't end up going to prison, but it got me kicked out of school. Didn't have the success my parents hoped for, but I did okay."

"And you ended up back here," Charley said. "Everyone seems to."

"Aye, it's a nice enough place, especially for the retirees. The holiday park keeps me busy but isn't too hard on me. Don't have anyone breathing down my neck – the wife does her bits and I do mine, and when it's quiet I sit out with a nice book or go fishing. Isn't really anything more a man could ask for."

"Let's go back a bit," said Thalassa. "You said there were stories about using magic to move goods."

Gordon scratched his head. "Right. Of course, they were all just stories to us, and not all of them were consistent. But as far as I remember, the idea was a ship would unload the contraband onto some offshore island, and they worked out a deal with the sea spider to move it to land."

"So Chelicerata includes sea spiders now?"

"It's not the literal Latin class," Gordon said, sounding frustrated. "It may not be closely related to any normal kind of spider, but in my book if it's got eight legs, it's a spider, and it made for a good name... Have you come across something like this, with all your sea magic stuff?"

"Not a sea spider specifically. But enough to make it believable. Extremely ill-advised, but believable."

"See, I know you do weird stuff. Magic, one might say. Granted, I've never seen you at it but you get results, far too often for me not to take it seriously."

Charley glanced at Thalassa. If yesterday's show didn't count as magic, what did? Thalassa shook her head, just a little, as Gordon continued.

"So I'm going to accept magic's a thing. But even then I find this one tough to believe. That said... there have been things going missing, drinks and snacks and stuff. While I was wearing the ring. So maybe..."

Charley held her breath, not believing what she was hearing. "If she got teleported out to sea using one of the rings, can't you just use yours to bring her back?"

"The ring never worked for me. Not for any of us who were still around in my day. I think they got us to try when we were initiated, but at the time I thought it was just part of the ritual."

"Artifacts like that rely on the user having a certain degree of innate magical aptitude to trigger them," Thalassa explained. "It's beginning to look like Melissa could be one of those people."

"So you could use it, then?"

"It's a dangerous thing to experiment with, Charley. I think we need to retrieve her the old-fashioned way. The last thing we need is all of us getting trapped, or worse."

Charley felt herself deflate. She turned back to Gordon. "So if we can't teleport her, do you know where this island they used to put stuff on is?"

"Only roughly, a bit north of here up the coast. Do you want me to talk to Lawson about getting his boat out?"

"Yes…" Charley started to say, but Thalassa raised her hand.

"Not today, I'm afraid. The weather…"

"We can't let that stop us! She needs rescuing."

"We don't have a choice. There's a storm coming in, a big one. Getting ourselves capsized and drowned won't do her any good, will it? Tomorrow, I promise."

From the dining hall of the holiday park, where she had been lurking because it had chairs and tables that made it easier for her to type and catch up on emails, than lying on the bed or having the laptop on her knee, Charley could see how the weather was changing. She gazed out through the window pane. The storm was coming in, as Thalassa had predicted. Gordon had, perhaps as some sort of peace offering, given Charley an extra blanket and some chocolate, and she had TV loaded up onto her laptop so she was feeling well prepared to ride this one out.

But then Gordon hurried back in, an anxious look on his face, and told her there'd been a warning that the river might flood. Everyone would need to be prepared.

Charley hurried to her car, took direction from a young woman in a hi-vis vest and gingerly drove along the road and on the track around the back of the holiday park. She gripped the wheel as she turned to place it in the narrow gap between two caravans. Near everyone was doing the same, getting the vehicles up to the highest ground they could and away from the banks of the river. Children were confined to their homes, and sandbags distributed, just in case, to the most low-lying houses. A place this isolated had no one else to rely on.

The dark clouds were gathering visibly, out to sea, and the wind was already gusting. All this and Melissa was trapped somewhere, maybe exposed somewhere that might be affected by the storm – perhaps devastatingly – and there was nothing, so far as she could tell, that Charley could do about it. She didn't ask if this was simple weather or something more, something – and she was scared to think the word – magical. She didn't feel like there was any point in asking anymore – the two worlds were increasingly becoming one, as if the distinction between magic and science was merely arbitrary, as if it just didn't matter to her how something happened, only that it did.

In the main grounds of the holiday park, Charley spent some time helping Therese gather loose items and put them in sheds, unhook the swings from their frames, lower and remove the flags at the entrance. Gordon was going round the permanent residents, checking they had what they needed. Charley paused, briefly, to watch him. His conversation with Thalassa showed he'd forgotten most of what had unfolded between them. Thalassa had admitted as much – denying it was anything she did, just that most people didn't have capacity to retain strong memories of magic. How much else were the people here forgetting?

She sighed, bringing her focus back to more immediate concerns. She considered her little wooden cabin with its thin walls, and just in case, made sure her things were packed away and put them in the dining hall which was much more securely constructed.

Sandbags were being transported in wheelbarrows and on small carts. Charley joined in, stacking them around the doors and ranch sliders of the houses of people she didn't know. As she hurried down to the shore, some more empty bags someone had found in a garage under her arms, she caught sight of Thalassa.

Thalassa was on the beach drawing much more intricate patterns than the ones she had made when Charley had first arrived, what seemed like a lifetime ago. Across them, she was laying lines of sea glass and coils of seaweed. Charley assumed she was somehow sheltering the settlement from the storm, but something about her demeanour looked almost as if she was inviting it in.

Charley wasn't sure she wanted to know, and she definitely wasn't going to ask Thalassa. Even if she wasn't so preoccupied. But she was intrigued by what she was doing, and, telling herself she'd run if it got bad, she stayed to watch, leaving the sandbags to a more burly local and clasping her coat around herself.

It began to rain seriously, heavy but perhaps not unusually so. It wasn't like Charley hadn't experienced a storm before – unlike almost everything else that had been going on recently, this at least felt within the range of normal calamities. She forced herself not to think about what it would be like for Melissa. There was nothing she could do about it, no way she could be found and, if need be, rescued, until the storm had passed, so it really wasn't helpful or sensible to put too much thought into it.

Thalassa was conducting rituals that made no overt sense but were spectacular to watch. She threw five shining objects into different points along the line of the shore, and they radiated a thin light from within the water. It was as if a protective wall or veil was being erected between the ocean and the settlement. The rain was doing nothing to wash away her sigils. Thalassa was small but she was a powerful presence standing there – the storm bringing in a cold light, the wind in her hair and her arms in her air, performing magic against the storm.

Charley was beginning to wonder how much of what Thalassa did was actually necessary for the magic, and how much was just for some sort of dramatic show. She definitely knew by now Thalassa put effort into looking like a magic practitioner, and while it was true she needed some support walking, a regular cane would probably have done quite well enough.

Unless she actually used that staff for magic, of course.

She wasn't the only one watching Thalassa, though others were clustered further back, not hiding exactly but not so exposed either. The storm raged out at sea and Thalassa seemed to hold it back, not putting it off entirely but directing it, managing it. It was windy and Charley couldn't tell if the water that splashed her face was rain or the wind whipping up seawater, but either way it wasn't as heavy as it had been earlier. She didn't quite feel she was dressed for the weather and had no idea why on Earth she would do it in any case, but nevertheless, she found herself walking forward towards the sea. The wind tugged at her hair and her clothes, but it was nothing to what lay ahead. Out there, by the waves, Charley watched as Thalassa worked with the storm.

Then she caught something from the corner of her eye, off to the left. She snapped her head round towards it, as if she knew before she saw it that she needed to react, needed to be on high alert. An amorphous shape among the clouds, undulating and turning from over the hills, perhaps mistakable for a cloud itself just by looking, but it came with other, impossible, dimensions. It carried a power that made Charley want to run, want to sink to her knees and curl up behind a rock, hoping it hadn't found her. Thalassa was holding up the whole sky, and if she'd noticed this she was in no place to deal with it.

It grew, coming towards the settlement; it was ugly and sickly, a yellow death glow filled with danger, and she backed away almost without realising it until she felt a wave break over her ankles. Charley didn't know how to deal with it but she raised her arms and gathered all her energy anyway. She stood firm even though it took all her will, even though it felt like something was trying to topple her over from all directions. She'd never felt so powerful but nor had she ever felt so small. And she unleashed the light. Blue hurtling into the air, as the storm rolled in. It was just beginner's magic, simple stuff, more show than substance. And this was hardly the time to be putting on a show.

But then Thalassa – who Charley could have sworn was far away down the beach only moments ago – was beside her. "Well done, child," Charley heard in her ear. "You're learning." And then the world went dark and cold and she was drowning.

Chapter Nine

The bed Charley awoke in was far comfier than her holiday park bunk – even though her whole body was aching and her head was throbbing, she could tell that much. The sheets were so soft it made her want to cry. Everything was eerily quiet. Another moment and she realised the pyjamas she was wearing were not her own. She tried to blink and look around but it was overwhelming, and she heard herself groan out loud. Her brain wasn't so much broken as it was completely full, unable to take in any new information.

"You awake, child?" came a voice. The room was dimly lit, and fortunately, no one thought now was the time to change that. Small mercies indeed.

Charley tried to reply, but she didn't think it emerged like any sort of coherent language. Nevertheless, in only a few moments, Thalassa was in the room beside her.

"I see you've woken. I'll get you some tea."

The last thing Charley wanted to be doing was making herself upright again to drink anything, let alone hot tea, but somehow, with the surprisingly gentle encouragement of Thalassa, she was sitting on the high bed with her legs dangling, drinking a cup of tea. It was less unpleasant than her previous medicinal tea experiences – it smelled, for want of a better term, more traditionally medicinal, and was a mid-brown colour. When she had finished it she felt both better – in the sense that she was in less pain – and deeply, deeply exhausted, as if she'd only just realised how fatigued she was. Putting the cup and saucer down on the bedside cabinet she swung her legs back into bed, sank into the mattress, and slept as if she had been awake for days.

Sunlight glowed through the curtains. Charley struggled to work out if it was morning, the same or a different day. Awkwardly rising in pyjamas that definitely weren't hers and yet fit her perfectly, Charley drew aside the curtains and looked out at the sea. The waters were calm and endless, the clouds clearing ahead of what looked like was shaping up to be a very nice day, but the beach and road were strewn with driftwood and debris.

"Morning," Thalassa said, pushing open the door gently.

"The storm...?" Charley asked, sitting back down on the bed. "What happened?"

"You slept right through it, I'm afraid. What do you remember?"

Charley felt like there was something much bigger than herself going on. And she didn't know how much to trust Thalassa with it – Thalassa who had taken seven years from her life. And now was not the time for processing a strategy. "Uh, just going down to the beach, I think," she lied.

"It was my fault. I'm so sorry. You got caught up in some of the magic I was doing and ended up falling in the water. It was nasty and cold, and I suspect you were already in a bad way because of all the stress you've been under. How are you feeling now?"

Charley struggled to think of an answer. To even grasp at the edges of what she'd experienced, and then to try to work out what Thalassa knew, and what she wasn't telling her... it all felt like too much. "Better?" she said tentatively. "A bit tired."

"That's to be expected. I've washed and dried the clothes you had on; let me know if I need to ask for anything to be brought over from the park."

Suddenly Charley felt so small and disconnected, the smallest in the universe she'd ever felt, as if she were a rag doll being thrown around in a huge warehouse or the back of a lorry, where there was so far to fall and nothing to cushion her.

"My phone," she said, distraught.

"It was in your pocket when you went into the water. I've put it in some rice. It was only in the water briefly, so hopefully it'll be okay once it's dried out. And before you look at me, no, I can't do magic on it, it would fry the internal processing unit. Magic can help you with a lot, but in this particular instance you're better off with rice. I'll check on it soon."

"Thanks," Charley said, feeling lost without it but not sure how to express that to Thalassa. There was nothing in particular she wanted to do online, she just needed the comfort of it. She wanted to be connected, to get in touch... "Melissa!" she cried suddenly, propelling herself off the bed. "We were meant to be going to find Melissa."

A wave of dizziness hit her and she sat back down abruptly on the bed. It seemed she was going to be little use to her sister or anyone else.

"Careful," Thalassa said. "Yesterday has drained us both." There was a kindness in her voice that Charley hadn't recognised before. "We're heading out as soon as we can, don't worry. I'm not letting you down."

Charley perched numbly on the edge of the bed, feeling overwhelmed by the fact that people – and Thalassa, in particular – were being so kind to her, when she had done so little to deserve it, hadn't really done anything as of yet, hadn't even had chance to show them she was properly a person, to prove herself to them.

"Thanks," she said. She searched to try to find a question that would help her understand what had happened. "Uh, what magic were you doing? Was it to protect Inver Aora from the storm?"

"That was part of it," Thalassa said slowly. "The part I'll tell most people, because even if they still don't believe me they'll at least believe my intentions were good. But mostly I was there to talk to the storm. To appease the forces within it and to hear what they have to say."

"By forces," Charley said. "Do you mean like spirits or gods or..."

"I mean forces of..." Thalassa stopped abruptly, pulling back the net curtain. "Looks like you've got a visitor. Would you like to borrow a house coat?"

True's face was all worry, all sadness, and it would be ridiculous to think that was just about Charley – someone she'd only known a few days. Charley was tempted to ask what was wrong, but instead she took the offered hand-sewn wheat pack and the chocolate and reassured her that she was fine.

True perched on a chair in the corner of the room. "I should have warned you this place can be dangerous."

"You kinda did," replied Charley, feeling her body swinging between hot and cold erratically.

"Clearly not well enough. I know it's pretty, and it's not *bad*, but it's just not like other places."

"And yet you all come back to it. I know, you have family here, but everyone seems to even though there's not much work. Even Anahera who everyone says was desperate to get away."

"Oh, we all said we hated it at that age. Let me take the wheat pack and put it in the microwave for you."

Charley felt the skin of True's hand brush against hers as she reclaimed the wheat pack, suppressed a gasp as something shivered through her. Something that wasn't anything to do with having been caught in a storm.

A couple of minutes later, True returned with the hot wheat pack and handed it back to her, then opened her bag. "I also brought some books. I don't know what you like, but if you get bored..." She passed over a small stack of battered paperbacks, what looked like a detective story and a romance and a couple of others.

"I really appreciate it, just this outsider turning up and everyone's been so kind to me."

"You're in trouble. Everyone's going to want to respond to that. It's okay, really. As long as..." – she pointed with her thumb to the next room – "...doesn't teach you to throw that blue lightning around or anything."

Charley chuckled nervously. "Oh, you remember that, then?"

"There are a few of us who see these things, even though they're hidden from most. Our families have been here a long time. Thalassa does her stuff and it's a bit weird, but she's given a lot to the community, especially when she was younger. Or so I'm told."

"You look after your own," Charley said, at once understanding, but feeling like she'd grown up in a place where that was an alien concept. More judging people on what church they did or didn't go to than looking after anyone. She felt herself relax and laughed along with True's chit-chat. She wasn't intimidating like she'd first seemed.

"*How* long have you girls been talking?" Thalassa asked from the doorway a while later, True's winter coat in her hand. True looked at her phone. "Ooops."

"Ooops indeed. You need to let this one get some rest."

True pulled on her coat and picked up her bag.

"Thank you again, I'll, uh, see you sometime," Charley said.

True waved from the doorway. "Take care of yourself!"

It was definitely magic that made her so uneasy about the idea of leaving this place behind, definitely magic and nothing at all to do with True. True was just someone she felt attached to because she'd been kind to her in difficult times, and she'd clung to that.

Definitely magic.

The Lawsons – well Anahera and her father, at least – were the next visitors, with Gordon showing up not far behind them, still awkward and a bit timid around Thalassa.

"I brought you some clothes. I didn't want to go through your things so I just grabbed a handful, I hope that's okay. And here's some lemon cookies Therese baked for you, and if you need any food or supplies just let us know."

Charley chatted with the group of them for a few minutes. Anahera was trying to talk about global warming and the increasing incidence of extreme weather events while their father desperately tried to shush them on the grounds it was not what Charley needed right now until Charley couldn't help but laugh.

When they'd gone she relaxed back into the bed, exhausted but secretly delighted that they had bothered. After resting quietly for 20 minutes, she pushed herself to get up, have a quick wash, and get dressed – just in time, as it turned out.

"More visitors," Thalassa called through the closed door, as Charley was pulling on her favourite hoodie. "Not sure we're going to enjoy these ones."

Charley emerged just as Thalassa was opening the door. Her heart sank and everything seemed surreal, like two entirely different worlds had somehow merged together and nothing made sense anymore.

"Charlotte, what – what *are* you doing out here? Is this another one of your games?" Her mother looked straight past Thalassa to address Charley directly, which suddenly and oddly struck Charley as rather rude. She was used to thinking of her parents as *the* standard for manners, with most other people, but in particular herself, continually falling short.

"Mum, Dad, uh, hi. Like I told you, I'm looking for Melissa."

"You're causing us both a lot of stress on top of everything. We had to drive all the way from Dunedin to this godforsaken place, and you haven't even been answering our messages – we even got Rupert to text you but it seems you're ignoring him too. Fortunately, one of the locals had the good sense to point us up here. Well? What have you got to say for yourself?"

"The phone was my fault," Thalassa said from beside the doorway. "It's being repaired now, and I've already given Charley my apologies."

"I am... so sorry my daughter's imposed on you," she replied, belatedly turning her attention to Thalassa. "We'll take her back to Dunedin right now. Maybe up to Tauranga – this supposed study clearly isn't working out."

"No." Charley tensed her muscles, trying to keep them from shaking.

"No?" her father asked, taken aback.

"No. I'm not going back to Dunedin with you. If I've outstayed my welcome here then Thalassa can tell me that, that's fine, but I have my car and another place to stay, and Inver Aora is the best place to find Melissa."

"You really think Melissa might have ended up out here?" Charley's mother asked, looking around in disbelief.

"Not here specifically," said Thalassa. "Sorry, we didn't get introduced properly. I'm a mostly-retired private investigator, I've worked with the police and other government agencies on forensic investigations. I'm well connected throughout Otago, and Charley and I are following several leads, including new information that has come to light from some of Melissa's colleagues. If you want to stay for some food I'd be happy to have you. You've come a long way and there's nowhere else to eat around here."

Charley's parents turned to each other. "Well," her mother said to Thalassa, "that would be very kind of you."

Thalassa hummed as she cooked, simple fettuccine with chicken and vegetables. Charley tried to set the table and quickly got dizzy, had to sit back on the sofa. She was feeling nauseous and she didn't think it was either her recent incident or being near the sea in general – no, this was a far older phenomenon, deeper-seated. She was scared of Thalassa learning the truth about her, of the conversation with her parents ending up revealing what she was really like.

Thalassa served the food, along with some garlic bread and more tea, sitting down at the table and finally helping herself. "You must be very proud of your daughter. She has her wits about her."

Charley almost choked in shock, avoiding making eye contact with either of her parents. She suddenly realised she was ravenous.

"Charlotte's always been the strong-willed one. The creative one of our children. She's got a great future ahead of her, she just needs to figure out which direction to head in."

There were barbs under every word, unmistakeably – Charley was more than used to that. But was she mistaken in also finding a note of pride, confidence, or at the least hope? It was probably just a show for Thalassa, she reasoned, them trying to look like reasonable and pleasant people, but was it possible that they thought she might turn out okay after all, that they hadn't entirely given up on her?

"I'm working on it, I promise," Charley said.

"We all had hiccups when we were young, didn't we," Thalassa said. "Fortunately life is long enough that they don't determine the rest of our futures. Now, I know it's very stressful but we have some good leads on Melissa, and we're going to head out tomorrow to look for her."

"What leads?" Charley's father asked suspiciously.

"I can't divulge my sources I'm afraid. But they are reliable."

Charley could see her father becoming angry, preparing to rise from his seat, but all of a sudden he appeared to think better of it, and settled back down to his meal. "Well... well I hope you're right."

They ate the rest of the meal in relative silence, Thalassa occasionally pointing out a bird flying past or sharing some fact about the area, and Charley's parents swallowing their annoyance to make small talk by asking about her paintings. It felt to Charley like it would go on forever, but eventually Thalassa was clearing away the plates and offering another cup of tea.

Charley's parents looked at each other.

"Is there somewhere in town we could stay? If you really think there's a chance of finding our daughter..."

"We'll have a boat ready to launch in the morning. If you follow the road just a little bit further you'll see the holiday park; Gordon's got a couple of cosy motel-style cabins where you'll be comfortable. And I'll make sure Charley gets plenty of rest so she's in a good place."

Charley watched her parents leave and felt like she was coming to the end of a journey. Soon everything would change. They would find Melissa – oh please, let her be alive! – and then Charley would go back to her old life, or to a version of it. Maybe she wouldn't stay in Dunedin, but she sure as hell wasn't going back to Tauranga. Either way, she would be back in a city. She would get a job and she might try to study again, if they'd let her. Her life would return to normal.

The people she'd met – the people she was starting to trust, Gordon's secrets notwithstanding – would become just blips in her life. Of course, she wanted to find her sister – she wanted to find her sister so badly she'd not only abandoned her life in Dunedin, but given up seven actual years of actual literal life. And yet there was a fear there, a terror that wasn't feeling like it was ever going to go away.

"I think they're what you young people would call intense," Thalassa remarked. "Not to worry, I got rid of them easily enough."

"You... you put a spell on my parents?"

"I used persuasion. Words, magic, didn't control them. If they'd really wanted to stay they'd have stayed, and within a couple of hours we'd all have lost the plot. Now, do you need anything else to eat? We want to get your strength up."

Charley was about to say *no thank you*, but Thalassa was already reheating crumble. It smelled good. She decided she wasn't going to complain.

"Are you using magic to keep me here?" she blurted out, all at once. "Like, have you cast a spell on me?"

Thalassa smiled, just slightly. "Do you really believe that? Ice cream?"

"Yes, please. And no, not really, but I keep meaning to go and get more groceries or new clothes, and... the only time it happened was when you took me, and I don't really understand why."

"Inver Aora wants you here, and you want to be here. Maybe not on the face of it – you miss your friends, you have a life – but on some level. You might be struggling to leave – you're probably also having issues with executive function, did you read up on that? – but that doesn't mean you can't. If it gets too bad I'll drive you to Dunedin and abandon you there myself."

Charley nodded, processing. "Thanks."

"Of course," she continued, "that's probably what I'd say if I *was* magically holding you captive here. It is the truth, but I'm afraid I can't give you more than my word for that."

Thalassa poured Charley another cup of tea, and she drank it without suspicion. Thalassa was hiding a whole lot, that was certain, but she didn't seem to be holding malice towards her. Of course, whether that was because she was basically a good person, or because she had some kind of use for Charley was yet to be determined.

Charley dug her spoon into her rhubarb and apple crumble. It was sharp and sweet at the same time, and she was surprised to find out how hungry she still was, and how it tasted of a childhood she wasn't sure if she'd ever really had. Probably too deep a thought to go with crumble. It was delicious anyway.

Chapter Ten

"I'm the one that has to do it?" Charley asked, in disbelief. "But I can't! I don't know what I'm doing, I can't even swim that well."

Thalassa sighed, shook her head, and filled up both cups of tea.

The settlement had been tidied, damage mostly repaired. Charley wished she'd been able to go down and help make herself useful, but Thalassa had told her she needed to save her energy. And now here she was having a meltdown about everything in this strange cottage.

"We have a boat, child. We're not asking you to swim the whole way. Just to guide us."

It might have technically been a vote of confidence, but it was anything but what Charley wanted to hear. She felt as if her feet were made of stone, as if she'd just been presented with an impossible task, with certain death, or with both. It wasn't a great feeling, really, and Charley had no idea where she was meant to take it. It wasn't about cowardice – at least she didn't think it was. It was that she needed the best possible person to look out for her sister, and Charley didn't believe that could possibly be her.

"I just... I don't have my life together. I can barely manage to find my shoes in the morning. I'm only coping now because I only have a few possessions with me. My flatmate has to handle the bills and harass me all the time for my share – in fact, I'm pretty sure I owe them at the moment and I've fucked up badly. I can't put my clothes away. I can't even keep track of what's clean and dirty and half the time I can't find clean underwear or socks. I fail out of uni. I get fired from jobs. I'm a fucking disgusting failure and it's bad enough you're going to see it because you think right now I'm not that bad. And I don't even care about my shame, you can think shit of me all you like but I am not okay with letting my lifelong failures kill the person I love most in the world. I gave you years of my life. Now you need to help me find my sister. You need to save her."

Thalassa drew in a long sip – well, more than a sip really – of tea and took a long hard look at Charley. She had the air of a parent revealing a long-held secret to a child. Charley forced herself not to physically recoil, but she did so mentally all the same.

"Charley, listen to me. I've hinted at it before but I've never said it explicitly. You have the same abilities I do. The same magic. You're the only person I've come across with them. I know other magic practitioners, of course, but no one who uses the sea in the same way, no one who responds to it and has the potential to engage with it in the way you can. Water fuels your magic, but it's also the main medium you can work through. If you're properly trained. If you put effort into studying."

Charley had so many questions she couldn't even start to pick one. She'd hoped she would find her sister, and instead, everything she thought she knew about herself was crashing down in ways that only a week ago she'd have thought to be literally impossible.

"So you taught me to make that blue orb – you said basically anyone could do that?"

"Yes, you've got me, I lied. It's not uncommon to have a bit of magic instinct, probably one in a hundred could manage that with enough training – most would need more than I gave you though. But you – you have far more. With the right instruction, you have so much potential."

"That's just the thing," Charley said, aware she was staring with her eyes wide, trying to process all this information. "I'm not trained at all. Unless you count telling me how to make a glowy thing, and glowy things aren't going to save my sister."

Thalassa shook her head. "Your powers are untrained and clumsy. But they're there. You are the only one who can save your sister, Charley. You understand, right, that your sister sent you that bracelet. The same way she stole those snacks from Gordon – loved how worked up he got over that, he thought he'd lost his senses. And there's a link between you. She has some magic or the ring wouldn't have done anything, but though it's most likely very weak, when it's combined with yours, you can connect. And you've made that connection. When you meditated on her bracelet, that established the line to her. You may not feel you know where she is, but you can find the way. I don't have that connection. It's up to you."

Charley steadied her hand on the back of the chair. "I don't know if I can do it. My brain. It's all muddled."

"It would have been better if we could have got you on some ADHD meds first. When you're not struggling so much with exhaustion from that magic might come a little easier. But I'm confident you can do it now."

Charley sucked in a breath, not sure she accepted Thalassa's faith in her but bowing out of the argument. "What about the thing in the storm?"

"You remember that, then? Don't worry, it's not going to come up this time. Just some trifling malicious entity trying to take advantage of my distraction during the storm; nothing you need to be concerned about right now."

Charley nodded, feeling unsteady. "I'm going to need some of that tea."

But Thalassa shook her head.

"You're going to need everything you have. Even if it hurts. Now get some shoes on. We're going to find your sister."

Soon, Charley would be leaving all this behind.

She emerged from the cottage slowly and carefully, not feeling 100% well, trying to keep herself upright and functioning as she went.

On her way down she took note of everything as though she wouldn't see it again. The arch of the roof and the seaweed hanging up underneath it. The few items of furniture in the courtyard and then the tight, winding path down, with the wall strung and decorated with rounded pieces of sea glass in blue and brown and green, and with pieces of driftwood, shorter than Thalassa used for her staff, and with fishing nets and lights and buoys and shells, so many shells, some flat light scallop shells and some that spiralled. The whole thing was at once a hoard and it was a work of art, it was a waste and yet it was perfect. Charley should have known the first time that there was magic here, and she had no idea how she could have missed it.

Never mind that now, though.

The boat ramp at the south end of Inver Aora's bay was the most basic example of such that could be functional, but it was enough. It felt like most of Inver Aora was here and it was oddly overwhelming, even for Charley who was used to much bigger crowds.

Thalassa handed Charley a keep-cup of ginger tea. "Helps with nausea," she said. "The best I can do in the circumstances."

Charley stood her distance from where her father was arguing with Lawson and another guy she didn't recognise about being allowed to go with them, and Lawson was having none of it. Still, her mother came up to her, fretting a little. Charley folded her arms inside her coat and nodded numbly.

Therese was fussing over her husband, seeking his reassurance he'd remembered various items. Others from the settlement had come to watch, some of the holiday park's permanent residents along with other vaguely familiar faces. Charley spotted Ollie at the front, excited by the occasion even though he probably didn't know what was going on. True, holding Allie behind him, reached out a hand and Charley took it.

"Good luck," True said, "I'll be thinking of you." Charley, suddenly teary and wordless, nodded her thanks.

The boat was a gleaming white, with bench seats at each side inside and outside the little cabin, maybe enough seating for 10 or 12 – plenty for this small group, anyway. The name 'The Codfather' was inscribed along the bow. Lawson helped Charley, Gordon, and Thalassa onboard. Lawson followed them onto the boat while his mate got back in the tractor and backed it down the ramp. The boat launched surprisingly smoothly from the trailer into the sea, Lawson started the engine, and then they were away.

Charley had rarely been on boats before – there'd been no practical reason to, and it obviously wasn't her idea of a good time. If she'd wanted to get between the islands she'd fly. Otherwise, it had only been when her parents or school made her, always a thoroughly miserable experience, and those years were behind her now. But now, though her heart was pumping fast with anticipation, she felt less uncomfortable than she'd feared.

The bay around Inver Aora was vast and wide which meant they were soon out into open waters. The wind wasn't up too heavy and thus even though it was a small boat the journey was relatively smooth.

"There are a few... well you could barely call them islands, but rocky outcrops northeast of here around where the shelf drops off," Lawson said. "I'm going to head for them unless you have any objections."

"Charley will tell you if you're heading in the wrong direction," Thalassa said. She passed Charley some tablets in a metallic sleeve. "You probably don't even know if you get seasick – regular seasick, not anything magical – so take one of these, and another if you feel you need it. They taste disgusting but we can't afford to have you incapacitated."

The pills did taste disgusting, but that was the least of Charley's concerns. Somehow, though, she did feel as if she would know if they were on the wrong track. For over an hour she said nothing, just sitting with the wind in her hair and the salt crusting on her skin, heading far out to sea, watching the land becoming smaller behind her, feeling the rocking of the boat. The winds became stronger and the water choppier, but she found it didn't bother her too much. Thalassa was standing dramatically at the rear of the boat, reaching out towards the albatrosses who circled her head astonishingly close.

Gordon chuckled. "Great fucking birds. Wouldn't want those shitting on my car windscreen."

Thalassa, of course, ignored him, and Gordon pointed out other birds that approached – the giant petrel (a bird that looked to Charley like it must be some relation to a dodo), the narrow-winged sooty shearwater – and told her about the sort of 19th Century whaling station that Inver Aora had started out as. If his intention was to distract her, Charley found it was more or less working – she was still anxious and uncomfortable, and her head was thumping, but she was holding things together far more than she would have expected.

A while later, something started to feel a little off. "I think you need to go a bit more northerly?" Charley suggested.

"Aye aye," replied Lawson, adjusting the boat's heading. "Does that look about right to you, Charley?"

Charley listened to her gut, something she was becoming better and better at doing. "I think so," she said. "I mean, it feels right."

Thalassa lowered her arms and the birds flew away.

"Spare pair of binoculars in that compartment there," Lawson said, pointing. "You want to get those. Keep looking. Don't let your mind get too used to what it sees otherwise it will just end up skimming over things."

Charley retrieved the binoculars and scanned the horizon with them.

None of them talked about what they were looking for. In the best case, it would be a dehydrated Melissa on a big rock. But they knew there was something... not entirely natural about her disappearance, and what they could end up finding... well, it went well into the impossible.

Soon Charley spotted rocks in the distance – they were dark as the sea was dark, but she could tell them most easily by the way the water splashed white against them. She pointed them out to Lawson, shuddering at the idea of her sister out here for over a week. Sometimes she caught a flicker, but when she moved the binoculars back it was only a wave or a bird, or her own hair flowing in front of her face – a good deal had made it loose from her ponytail at this stage of the operation.

"Gonna get a bit closer and then we can go back and forth if it's round here."

"Thanks," said Charley. She felt sick, like something heavy had landed in her stomach. It wasn't sea sickness. This was the hour when they would either find Melissa safe and well or they would have nothing else left to try. There didn't seem to be any middle ground.

The islands were tiny, the largest among them no more than a few metres across, circled with jagged rocks. The water broke against them, spraying high into the air, while below treacherous foam swirled back and forth.

Charley scanned them methodically through her binoculars, one at a time. The sun was harsh on her, and she'd had to put her sunglasses away so she could use the binoculars better. Her T-shirt was soaked and water was running down her face like tears. "She's not there," Charley whispered. "She's not there."

Everything was lost. She couldn't find Melissa and she couldn't face going back.

"Focus, child," said Thalassa. Charley tried – she tried her best – but there wasn't even a reason for it anymore and her brain was all over the place, swirling everything from the past week: Melissa's disappearance, yes, but this whole town. Thalassa. True. Magic. Magic was real and she had magic. And the sea didn't really make her ill, it just awakened her magic which was too much to process because she had other issues going on with her mind. There was the beach, and the rocks, there were packets of noodles in the holiday park kitchen, the teens that hung out by the river, the houses staggered up the hill on the other side.

"What do you want me to focus ON?" she yelled above the noise of the waves and the idling engine. Dunedin. Her tiny room that barely fitted a bed – did her rent go out? Had the sour cream in the fridge expired and would anyone have thought to clean it out?

"CHARLEY."

The boat was rocking and she was distressed and her mind all over the place, but somewhere in herself she found it, like a glowing thread she caught and clung to, reeling it in.

"There," she cried, pointing. There was another island, substantially bigger than the other tiny rocks in the group, and something – or someone, even – atop it.

"How the hell did we miss *that*?" Lawson asked. "We must have gone right past it." He pulled the boat around. Gordon rubbed his eyes and stared out towards the island. Charley raised the binoculars and turned the wheel to adjust the focus. A woman, stretched out on the rocks – not close enough to tell if it was Melissa, but surely it must be – with silvery strands all over her.

But the boat wasn't getting any closer. She turned to look at Lawson, who was wrestling with the wheel. "What's wrong?"

"I, uh, can't seem to steer the boat in the right direction."

"Can you try increasing the power to get through the waves?" Gordon suggested.

"Yeah, thanks for that. Tried that and everything else obvious. It's not just the waves. Something is blocking me."

Charlie could somehow feel Melissa almost as much as she could see her. She remembered what Thalassa had said; Melissa only had weak magic, but the two of them had a connection. That it was up to Charley to save her.

"It's not working," Lawson said, above the noise of the motor which was being pushed to its limits. "Do you want me to go around and try from a different angle?"

"No," Charley said, taking off her shoes then her jeans, shivering in underwear and a T-shirt. "Just stay here as best you can." She blocked out the sounds of Gordon trying to call her back and Thalassa holding him off, and looked down into the ocean depths she'd hated all her life. Then she took a deep breath and plunged into the water.

It was shockingly cold. She'd never swum in open seas like this before, but she had retained enough from childhood swimming lessons to keep herself afloat, and managed to strike out towards the island. She felt a barrier in the air and the water, a sort of thickening like she was swimming through oil, but Melissa was ahead of her and she pushed through it.

"Watch out!" Lawson yelled behind her. Then Charley saw it, like a great dome rising out of the water in front of her, an undersea explosion, all in slow motion. The waves tossed her like a toy, and she barely managed to keep her head above water.

It continued rising, water falling from it and then dripping down, until it was clear it wasn't one dome but eight raised segments.

Eight legs, thin and impossibly long, rising and rising now, a pale yellow-brown, a creature many times larger than the boat, and its body, what Charley supposed must have been its face, looking straight at her. There was something about it that felt like it wasn't part of this world, something that reminded her of the entity that had come with the storm, but it was undeniably there, solid and threatening.

Its great legs, easily twice Charley's height to the knee, and then that again to the body, just brushed the water, skating on the surface. It pulled back, straddling the island, towering above the rocks, towering above Melissa. The waters began to calm. The creature leaned its body forwards as if inspecting Charley.

She treaded water just in front of it. She was so close. She could see the silk draped over Melissa was filled with swirls and curves, reminding her of sigils Thalassa worked out on the beach. She looked exhausted and her cheeks hollow, and her eyes were closed, but her hair fanned out in a way that made her look angelic.

Charley forced herself to look up. She could see the segments of the sea spider's eyes, see its fangs above her. She didn't mind admitting to herself that she was terrified.

Incredibly, the spider spoke. "You came for her?" it asked, raising one leg until it pointed at Charley's chin. Its voice was like nothing Charley had ever heard before, quivering at a frequency she felt like she shouldn't be able to hear.

"She's my sister," Charley replied, forcing confidence when actually she wanted to curl up in a ball and never look at that creepy, pointing leg again. "She needs to come back home!"

"I honour the bargain," the spider said.

"What bargain? Please let her go. She belongs with me."

"So young," the spider chittered, every word vibrating. "Even the young must keep the bargains."

"What do you want from us?" Charley yelled. She was shivering in the cold and all her muscles felt exhausted just from keeping afloat.

"You want everything moving. Back and forth, back and forth. I protected what you sent, protect it still."

Charley stared at the spider. "So you don't want to hurt her?"

"Why hurt humans? Can't eat you. Would only hurt if necessary to protect."

"When do the goods stop needing protection?" Thalassa yelled over the wind.

"When they send for them! With the rings, they call for them, I transport them."

"But no-one knows how to use the rings anymore," said Charley. "Please, she wasn't sent here for protection, it was all a mistake! She's my sister and she needs to come home now."

"I have to protect her."

The vibrations of the spider's voice were ringing in Charley's ears. "Look, Gordon has a ring, show them, Gordon. See, she's ours, and we're here to claim her."

"If you have the ring, then summon her."

"I just told you! Argh." Charley tried to focus, tried to calm herself down. Her sister was *right there*. She was almost tempted to try to fight this giant sea spider for her, but that was the way people got killed. Killed and made into memes. And a quick look back at Thalassa confirmed there was no magical way out.

"Look, you say you want to protect her but she's not in good shape. She's all pale and so thin."

"Thin for a human. Not for one of us. Humans are weak."

"Humans are not designed for the sea. If you entrust her into my care I will take her where her needs can be met. Where it is the right temperature for her and she has fresh water and the food she can eat."

The spider paused and swung its body forwards on its legs to be close to Charley. "Do you lie?"

"No. No, I swear it. There's nothing I want more than to protect my sister."

"If you wanted to hurt her you would say the same."

"I would, but look. You can see the state she's in now. Please. Is there a way I can prove to you I'm not lying?"

A single strand of silk drifted down towards her from the spider. Instinctively, Charley caught hold of it, leaning her head against it.

"We catch thoughts with this. Maybe one of yours will be satisfying. Show me how you protect her."

Magic, thought, memory. The boundaries between the three were not clearly defined, and Charley was searching through all of them. It was easy to find times Melissa had looked after her, protected her, and taken care of her, and so hard to find the opposite. God, she'd been a difficult child, didn't understand why Melissa still wanted anything to do with her.

"Charley, stop it." Thalassa's voice pierced the air. "Don't get into that pattern. You need to find the right sort of thoughts."

They came, slowly and awkwardly. Charley, making brownies for Melissa's birthday. Charley, spinning extra on the flat cleaning wheel when Melissa was busy with revision. Charley, bringing home supplies from work when Melissa was ill. Charley, telling her jokes when she was exhausted from studying. Charley...

Eventually, she heard the words: "released, released to your protection", and she fell back utterly drained.

The spider leapt into motion, all its legs working together in some terrifying choreography as it skittered away across the sea impossibly fast, dancing off past the horizon.

"What," said Charley, "the fuck. Was that?"

But even as she said it she was clambering onto the island while the silk that had been restraining her sister melted into nothing. Melissa lay there with a scattering of empty bottles and wrappers around her, wet and pallid but alive. She was half-waking now, her eyes flickering, and behind her Charley could hear the engine of the boat approaching.

"I'm here, Melissa," she said, taking her sister's hand. "We're going home."

Chapter Eleven

Back in Dunedin, everything went by in a haze. Melissa was in hospital for a couple of days – as a patient for a change – for what she described dismissively as fluids and rest. Privately, one of the nurses took Charley aside and said it was a wonder she'd survived, that she was in such good shape given what she'd been through.

As soon as her sister was discharged, Charley picked up extra work shifts, to return favours and because she was basically out of money. Their mother was hovering around the flat taking care of Melissa, and as there was no real way to save her sister from it, Charley was just glad to be out of her way. She told the few friends she happened to see that things had been so stressful that she'd rather not talk about it, but she really appreciated the support they'd shown her. She was hoping that made sense to them, because the truth certainly wouldn't, and the other truth was that she was simply exhausted. She slept much of the time and felt dazed even when awake, replaying video games she knew well and didn't have to think through too carefully.

Something was changing in her, something she didn't know how to explain. She felt like she was at a crossroads and suspected either she would go back to Inver Aora forever or she would never see it again, and right now, at this point in time, both of those choices seemed utterly unbearable.

Within a week, Melissa was already looking much better – she got a haircut, and her cheeks were filling out. She filled in the details for Charley, lying on the sofa while Charley sat on the floor below, throwing a rice-filled frog toy from hand to hand.

"It was such a silly thing," Melissa said. "I went back to look for the ring, and then just as I found it someone charged in with an emergency, a car crash I think, so several people all at once, all with likely fractures, and it was all hands on deck. And then... I don't even know how, I forgot until I was at home, and I was just answering a few emails before bed, and I found it in my pocket, couldn't believe I'd forgotten. And I was really panicked about it, about to text my supervisor and then, bam, I was on an island in the middle of the ocean."

"With a giant spider," Charley added.

"Holy shit that thing. I thought I was hallucinating. Going to be nicer to the regular-sized ones, they don't seem so scary now. But... y'know, the first few days, I was just sitting on the island. And after a while these things... these things kept appearing. Like a chocolate bar when I was hungry. A bottle of water when I was thirsty. I suppose I was summoning them with the ring. But it seemed very strange."

"Well, I'm glad you did. Water especially."

"And it was only later the spider put all the weird silk over me. I think it might have helped in some way, not just keeping me restrained. I mean, it wasn't like there was anywhere I could go! I don't remember much after that." She sat up and stretched. "Do you fancy a walk, just down the street to get coffee? I think it will do me good."

Charley forced her feet into her still-laced-up shoes. Things seemed both very normal and very abnormal all at once. They got their drinks and sat on a bench round the corner.

"So, uh, Thalassa suggested I see a doctor," Charley said, at last, sipping her iced tea even though November in Dunedin was still not the weather for it. Tentatively, she told Melissa about the psych appointment and Thalassa's hypothesis, and about the forms needing to be completed by someone who knew her as a child.

"Huh," said Melissa, squinting at Charley. "You know, that would make a lot of sense. I don't know much about it, though."

"It's okay, this psych dude is the professional. It's more questions like, when Charley was a child, were they in trouble for daydreaming a lot?"

"Well, that's easy..." Melissa said. "Sorry."

Charley forced a smile. "It's true, though. Hey, what are you going to do about missing your exams? Will you still be able to qualify?"

"Yeahhhh, I'm still hoping for some sort of dispensation that will allow me to take them without repeating the year. It's a bit difficult when I can't explain what happened, but the police are calling it a situation beyond my control which they're still investigating, which actually helps, believe it or not. So fingers crossed. But either way, I'll get there in the end."

"I hope they sort something out..."

"Honestly," Melissa said. "I mean, so do I, but I'm also feeling oddly relaxed about the outcome. It feels like things are just going to fall into place one way or another, you know? And if takes me an extra year, well I think there are some new things I can learn. Things that seemed so important just a little while ago just *aren't* that much. So much stuff out there that I didn't even know I didn't know."

"I've been thinking of going back to uni too?" Charley said, hesitantly.

"Oh yeah?"

"Yeah. I've been thinking. If this ADHD really is why I've been finding things so hard – and I think it is, I really do – then there are things I can do about it. I might be able to get through uni. Be more organised. Hold down a proper job. Just remember to brush my hair more consistently. I could be everything I'd always dreamed about being."

"Were those *your* dreams, though?" Melissa asked gently, and Charley began to cry, horrified at herself, hot tears that somehow wouldn't stop coming.

"I just wanted to not be terrible." Charley felt Melissa's arm around her shoulders, let herself be pulled in close.

"You've never been terrible. I promise you. And if you really want to study, or have a career in mind that needs a degree, then of course, and I'll try to do more to support you. But I don't think that's the best place for you."

Charley dried her eyes. "Why not?" she asked, trying to sound as normal as possible.

"You know I used to read heaps of books as a kid?" Charley nodded. Melissa had been an *advanced reader*. She'd heard about that from an early age. "Well I read lots of books about children going through magic portals, and I used to think about what would happen if one opened when we were playing or on our way back home from the pool, and do you know what I always felt?"

Charley shook her head, feeling something bitter rising in the back of her throat. She let Melissa continue.

"I felt jealous of you. Because I knew you were the one with the courage to go through, the one who would have the adventures. That deep down I was too boring and too scared for that."

"You're not boring!" Charley exclaimed, indignantly.

"Maybe not boring exactly. But I tread well-worn paths. I'm not upset about it, it's just who I am. But you... you're extraordinary. It's not because you do or don't have ADD, and it's probably not even because you have magic. It's your personality. You're curious. You talk to people even when it scares you. You can do things that no one would have thought possible. Don't pass up this opportunity. It's your chance to be who you really are. Not a lot of people get a chance like that handed to them."

"Mum and Dad are going to think I've finally failed them for good," Charley replied.

"Let them."

Charley realised her sister's voice was forceful and seething with barely contained rage. She felt suddenly cold, and, if she could be excused the pun, rather all at sea. "I'm sorry, I know you have a good relationship and I'm glad, but..."

"No." Melissa's response was firm. Charley blinked in confusion.

"No, you don't have a good relationship?"

"Well no, I don't. But I mean, if people treat you like crap, don't feel you have to be okay with it just to keep them happy. You understand? It's ultimately your life. I know this sounds clichéd, but. It's honestly true."

Charley found what she was hearing difficult to comprehend. "I failed them at every turn. But they worshipped you???" she said, trying not to sound as surprised as she felt. "You were exactly the child they wanted, their golden child. You did everything right."

Melissa looked pained, and Charley's instinct was to apologise, even though she didn't know what she might have said wrong, to try desperately to make it all stop, but before she could decide how to proceed, Melissa took a deep breath and resumed talking.

"Okay, let me tell you a story. It's not a nice story but you're ready for it. So, when I was 15 or 16, a couple of years at least until uni, I was struggling with... well with a lot of things really, and the school wanted me to drop some of the extras, for my own well-being as much as anything else. They worked out what I needed to get into first-year health science and what I could drop, and it was going to make things so much easier on me and let me take a breather while still meeting all my goals. The school presented this to my parents. And they said no. And at this point I was in a really bad way, not eating properly, self-harming, trying desperately to get control of everything. And they just... didn't care about what was best for me. They cared about me fulfilling a role for them. I got through, but it was the worst year of my life, and honestly, it could have killed me. So I know it was worse for you. I know you bore the brunt of it and they were cruel to you in a way Rupert and I didn't experience. But if you think they were happy with me as I was... that wasn't the case."

Charley looked at her sister, feeling like there was a whole rush of information, whole years of experiences she'd had, now queuing to be re-evaluated, flooding her. "Why..."

Melissa shrugged. "Because they liked having images of children more than they actually liked having real people as children? Because they'd gloated to all their friends about me being in all these pro-grammes and they couldn't take it back? That was their concern. Not my well-being, not in the slightest. But once they find out that I'm not okay with it, that I'm not going to be married and give them grand-children, that I'm not this picture of normative success, well, let's just say the love you've seen them display to me isn't unconditional."

"You're... not going to marry? Like just not going to *marry* marry or you're not going to be with anyone?"

"You know I've never really dated, right? And definitely never been in a relationship?"

"I thought you were just busy with study."

"I thought that too. I didn't really have any other explanation for myself. And then when I worked it out I kept pretending, because it was easier than being dismissed or told I was just being childish or making things up. But the truth is that I've never been interested. I've never got it. At first, I thought I was just a late developer, but then I heard words like asexual and aromantic and realised they applied to me. But it was easier to pretend I was focused on study – which wasn't untrue – than to try to explain that."

"So all that looking at magazines together when we were teens… oh shit, did I put pressure on you to fake that?"

"*You* didn't. I was faking to myself, but it was fun sometimes too. I can find people pretty. The way I can find nice curtain fabric pretty. But whatever it is that pings in most people, that attraction, it just doesn't happen for me. I honestly don't know what it would be like if it did, but I don't feel like I'm missing out."

"You know, they didn't totally freak out when they found out I was bi. They weren't happy, but they didn't, like, disown me or anything. But maybe they just always expected me to be weird."

"I'm sorry, it sounds horrible to say, but yeah. For me, it would be the whole golden-child façade crumbling, and they'd be desperately trying to build it back up. There'd be sobbing and late-night phone calls, and the only way I'd be able to cope would be to cut them off, and then that would have financial implications. It's cowardly, I know, and very selfish, but being able to start out without a big student loan hanging over me is worth it. Probably. But once that's over there's going to be some distance between us, and either they start making some changes or I stretch that distance even further. It's not about punishing them, it's about living my own life and not being sucked into all the drama every time."

Melissa would be okay, though. Maybe not everything was how it had seemed with her, but she was strategic, in control of things. And she wanted to be family for Charley, and both of them could dispense with their parents and anyone who took their side and still have each other. Melissa had a plan, and it was time for Charley to make hers.

But it was not a plan, returning to Inver Aora. One day she just did it, everything seeming to come together so easily and naturally. She took food with her this time, a full suitcase of clothes, her consoles; packed up the car, and drove. The nausea, the disorientation, the general malaise of it all hit later this time, not until she could actually see the sea and taste the salt in the air, but it was still strong. She didn't even need to drive as far as Thalassa's house; the woman was standing by the road, with the wind incoming from the sea blowing out her hair dramatically. Charley pulled over and got out – it wasn't a good place to park, but she knew by now just how little traffic came through here. Thalassa handed her a metal flask, one of the ones where the lid doubled as a cup.

Charley knew before she opened it that it would be the weird tea. It had never actually reached appetising levels, but it no longer repulsed her – instead she just ignored the smell and taste. Even after a few sips, she was starting to feel better.

"Someone who hates the sea having sea magic. What an irony," Charley said, her eyes fixed on the horizon. Summer had returned. Inver Aora was busier now – children were exploring the rocks for pools and crabs, tourists were walking the beach. Charley didn't mind a bit of busyness. In fact, it made the place feel more attractive, knowing that at least for a few months every year it wouldn't be quite so isolated, that there'd be new people to talk to.

"It's not a coincidence. It's not being able to focus your magic, the whole overwhelming power of the thing that you don't have the mental resources to conceptualise. It doesn't matter. It's still clear to me that you have a similar sort of magic to what I have, just buried. I suspect it's... it's not even the ADD that's obscuring it, so much as the amount of effort and pressure you're putting yourself under to try to compensate for it. You're exhausted, poor child."

Charley wanted to burst into tears then and there. She was exhausted, she always had been, and it felt like no one else had even noticed. She held her composure, though. Dramatic displays of emotion really weren't Thalassa's thing.

"I don't know how to use it, though," she said.

"That's okay. You went to Dr Pedrick, as I suggested?"

Charley nodded. "Yep, and I'm going to be paying him off for the rest of my life. Closest thing anyone my age is going to get to a mortgage. But... you were right. ADHD inattentive type. He prescribed me some meds, and recommended some books."

"And it's helping?"

"Yes..." Charley replied cautiously. "I mean, it's not a miracle. And the pills have some side effects, and sometimes things get worse when they wear off. But... wow. I've realised I was dealing with so much more than other people. No wonder I found it hard."

"Indeed."

"I... uh, thank you for telling me. I don't know yet how it affects the sea thing. I didn't... I mean the doctor knows about magic, right, but I still didn't want to bring it up."

"He does, but you made the right decision. That's not part of his job. We'll figure out if ADHD or something else has been overwhelming you. Once that's dealt with, some of it will come naturally. Most of mine I figured out through trial and error, but you don't have that long, and in any case, your generation is too impatient. So. Do you want to stay in Inver Aora and learn to use your power?"

"I..." Charley began.

"It will be intense. You can have the studio. It doesn't have electricity, but it does have a bathroom, and we can try running a cable or something. It's going to be hard work. You'll get a cut when people pay cash. But there's not much to spend your money on here, is there?"

"Do I get the seven years of my life back?"

"Ha! No, I'm afraid not, but you might learn enough to take a different seven years from somewhere else. But I do have something for you. It will help you focus your power as you learn to grow it."

The pendant was a soft, muted blue – it might have been sea glass, or it might have been something else entirely, well-worn and rounded by the sea. Charley put it on, awkwardly adjusting it around her hoodie until it sat comfortably. Charley could feel the power but it wasn't overwhelming – it was warm and nurturing. She turned, and the water in front of her was filled with possibility. Charley looked out to sea.

Writing may be more solitary than other practices, but no book is made alone. Thanks to everyone on the Slacks and at the Pub, and to the Saturday half-price-mimosas folk, for support, direction, vent-space, and more. Thank you to the Witchy Fiction crew for setting me on this path. Thank you to Jacqueline Sweet for once again making me a great cover. And particular thanks to Emma, Jackie, and Kelly for their work in helping me make this book the best I could make it.

If you enjoyed *Tides of Magic*, keep an eye out for the second book in the series, *Tides of Change*, out later in 2023.

Andi R. Christopher writes queer urban fantasy (where urban is sometimes a small town, but always somewhere mysterious things happen) set mostly in Aotearoa New Zealand. They're a fan of weird sea creatures, strange plants, and hidden magic. Andi also writes other kinds of science fiction and fantasy (still sometimes with weird sea creatures) as Andi C. Buchanan.